CAMP CHALLAH

NOAH GREEN
SAVES THE
WORLD

NOAH GREEN
SAVES THE
WORLD

Laura Toffler-Corrie
illustrated by Macky Pamintuan

KAR-BEN
PUBLISHING

KAR-BEN PUBLISHING®
An imprint of Lerner Publishing Group, Inc.
241 First Avenue North
Minneapolis, MN 55401 USA

Website address: www.karben.com

Main body text set in Bembo Std regular.
Typeface provided by Monotype Typography.

Library of Congress Cataloging-in-Publication Data

Names: Toffler-Corrie, Laura, author. | Pamintuan, Macky, 1976– illustrator
Title: Noah Green saves the world / by Laura Toffler-Corrie ; illustrated by Macky
    Pamintuan.
Description: Minneapolis, MN : Kar-Ben Books, [2020] | Audience: Grades 4–6 |
    Summary: Twelve-year-old aspiring filmmaker Noah stumbles his way through the
    summer at a Jewish sleepaway camp while his elderly grandfather is sending him
    messages by carrier pigeon about saving the world.
Identifiers: LCCN 2019026096 | ISBN 9781541560369 (library binding) |
    ISBN 9781541560376 (paperback)
Subjects: CYAC: Camps—Fiction. | Friendship—Fiction. | Grandfathers—Fiction. |
    Motion pictures—Production and direction—Fiction. | Jews—Fiction. | Spies—
    Fiction.
Classification: LCC PZ7.T57317 No 2020 | DDC [Fic]—dc23

LC record available at https://lccn.loc.gov/2019026096

Manufactured in the United States of America
1-46296-47171-3/12/2020

TO MY PARENTS, HINDA AND ALVIN.
FOR SEEING ME.
AND, ALSO, FOR CAMP.
—L.T.C.

CHAPTER 1

An early summer breeze wafts through my window, and I hear the growling motor of the Shady Pines Retirement Home van crawling slowly up our tree-lined street. As it makes a careful turn into our short driveway, I happily shove as much stuff as I can into my lumpy duffel bag.

Super exciting things are about to happen!

For one, in just a few short hours (forty-two to be exact), I'm almost ninety-five percent sure that I'll be going to the David Lynch Film Camp in Los Angeles.

Even though I'm only in seventh grade, this is a big deal for me because I want to be a film-maker. Not the kind who just tells stories. But the kind who *observes* stories. I want to create my life opus, a very big story, in a style called *cinéma vérité*, a term I learned in Mr. Burns's after-school film club. Mr. Burns says *cinéma vérité* reveals not only the truth in other people, but the truth in oneself.

This sounds like a good thing for me because people confuse me sometimes. As for revealing the truth in myself, I'm not exactly sure what that means. I'm guessing it's that thing where you say or do something and then afterwards you're like, "That was stupid. Why did I say that? And why are people looking at me like I smell bad or something?"

So by observing others, maybe I can cut down on those types of experiences because, if I'm being honest, that kind of happens to me a lot.

Plus, for Hanukkah, Aunt Bea got me this awesome headpiece camera, which is very cool because I can film people even from far away. The only problem is that I almost got punched once by a kid who thought I was spying on him, which was not my intention. But Mr. Burns says good art should be dangerous, so maybe I'm on the right track.

As for the David Lynch Film Camp, I say I'm only ninety-five percent sure I'm going because, at first, my parents weren't hot on the idea. They were like, "Sorry. Not happening. It's too far away and too expensive."

But I can be really persistent when I want something. So I started talking it up, like, all the time, at every meal, during every car ride, during TV shows. But then I noticed Mom and Dad were kind of avoiding me, so I thought: go subtle. I started leaving brochures around the house in places I knew they'd look, like inside the refrigerator crisper bin, plastered across the car windshield, and taped to the lid of the toilet seat.

Although that might have been a little overkill because at one point Dad was like, "Mention that camp one more time . . ." Then he didn't finish his sentence, which meant he was really mad.

Eventually, he said he and Mom would think it over, which gave me hope. That is until my sister, Lily, reminded me that sometimes that means they've already made up their minds and they're never gonna do it.

But last night, they told me to pack my bags. For a second, I thought they were kicking me out. Lily said I wasn't reading the room right, which, as I said, is kind of my problem. They promised there was a good surprise coming. So now I'm really stoked. Lily's also stoked because she thinks that means she can do what she wants to do this summer too.

The second exciting thing that's going to happen has to do with my Pops. Today is his birthday party. We think he's turning ninety-something, though Pops refuses to say. Yesterday he sent me a mysterious email, saying he has a secret that will change my life forever. I can't imagine what that is, but I bet it's cool!

So, right now, I'm going to find out his big secret. I'm going to make sure I get a hard "yes" from Mom and Dad about film camp. And I'm going to record everything on my camera, which I'm securing firmly around my head as I make my way down to our living room for the party Mom is throwing for Pops.

Pops's friends from Shady Pines are already milling around, filling their paper plates with salad and lasagna. Festive party decorations dot the room, and silver tinsel bristles hang across the fireplace mantel. Mom's large picture board of the history of Pops's life, family, and friends is propped up on the table. Stretched across the archway to the living room is a purple papier-mâché banner that reads: *Happy Whatever Birthday, Pops!*

Lily pops in front of me, looking annoyed. "Noah! Where were you? We need more cups." She leans in close. "Rabbi Blum's had like twelve cups of coffee already, and he keeps leaving them everywhere."

She stomps away.

I spy Rabbi and Mrs. Blum by the buffet. He's probably the most energetic rabbi we've ever had at Temple Beth Israel. He's chatting and bustling around while helping spoon food onto one of the old people's plates.

Lily likes to say that I'm the exact opposite of what she wanted in a brother if she could have picked. Good thing she couldn't! But the fact is that nobody gets to pick. Sisters. Parents. Or even ourselves. Not being able to choose ourselves is probably a good thing, though, because we would most probably never pick who we are and then who would we be?

Pops ambles by me.

"Happy birthday, Pops," I say. "How old are you exactly again?"

"None of your beeswax," he grumbles.

"Hey," I continue, "what's that secret you emailed me about?"

"Can't tell you now, Ned," he says, calling me the name he wanted my mother to give me, after his uncle on his father's side, but she liked Noah better.

"Noah," I say, even though he's not really paying attention and is already on to another subject.

"That nosey dagnabbit doctor is listening to everything I say," Pops huffs and shuffles away.

Dr. Marchant, the resident MD at Shady Pines, snoozes loudly in a nearby chair.

Just so I wouldn't be totally bored, I've invited some of my friends from school. I don't have a lot of friends like Lily does, but my closest friends from film club showed up: Bailey, who has thick glasses, straggly hair, and a T-shirt that reads, *Save the Dolphins*. And Rex, who's got straggly hair and the beginnings of a very skimpy goatee. His T-shirt says: *Save the Filmmakers*.

"Hey guys!" I wave.

Bailey waves back then stares out the window, and Rex scratches down the back of his shirt with a plastic fork.

They rock!

And speaking of friends, there's my new friend, Simon. I noticed him yesterday on the school bus, looking a little lost. Principal Lefrak said that he's an exchange student from London, so I figured I should take him under my wing. He might even be a good candidate for film club. I'm sure he's feeling very out of place away from home.

"Hey Simon," I wave, but he's whispering into his phone.

"Yes, I'd like to leave," Simon says.

At that moment, Mom carries out Pops's birthday cake, which is decorated with so many candles she has to blink from the smoke and flames.

"*Happy birthday to you!*" Mom breaks into song.

All his friends join in until the song peters out from general lack of enthusiasm.

"Pops, you want to cut the first piece?" Mom asks.

Pops frowns and stares into the cake. "You know that butter icing gives me the bathroom hoppies. And who's Mel?"

Mom makes a sharp cut into the cake. "That's you, Pops."

"No one ever calls me Mel," he grumbles. "They call me by my nickname."

"Now, you know you don't have a nickname." Mom smiles tensely.

"Yes I do! Don't tell me I don't have a nickname," he insists. "It's Liplock Field. I was a secret agent for the CIA, and I always kept my mouth closed! But now almost everyone I know is dead . . ."

He looks over at his friends, waiting, empty plates in their hands.

"Or will be soon."

"Now Pops." Mom gently places her hand on his shoulder. "You were a lieutenant in the army, and then you worked in insurance for thirty years. You know you were never a secret agent."

"That's because it was a secret!" he snaps.

"Hey Mom," I say. "So what's my surprise news? Can you tell me now?" I adjust my headpiece into her face for full cinematic effect.

"A little busy here, Noah," Mom says with one of her tight-lipped, aggravated expressions, as she makes her way toward the kitchen.

I follow her. "Where's Dad? Can he tell me about—"

"Ned! I need to talk to you." Pops steps into my path.

"In a little bit, Pops. I'm trying to get my big news," I say, tapping my camera headpiece, "and I'm getting footage for my opus."

"You've got pus?!" Pops shouts, holding a fork aloft like a dagger. "Just hold still. One good poke and it'll all come oozing out. You'll be as good as new."

Lily dives in and gently extracts the fork from Pops, just as Dad appears, up in my face.

I brighten. "Hey, Dad, are you gonna tell me my surprise now?"

"Noah, did you rake the wet leaves off the front steps like I asked you?!" he says. "Your Uncle Larry will try and sue us if he slips again."

"Ned, I think I've got the bathroom hoppies," Pops announces, grabbing my arm and pulling me around the corner into the laundry alcove.

Suddenly he's all secretive. "I need to talk to you. It's very important."

"But I thought you had the bathroom hoppies."

"Forget about that." He leans in and wiggles his wiry eyebrows. "The thing is that—"

"Can it wait?" I interrupt, eyeballing the kitchen. "I'm hoping for some promising news . . ."

"I don't think so," he says, leaning in closer. He's so close now that his eyebrow hairs are tickling my forehead, and he's like, "You have to help me save the world."

CHAPTER 2

"Huh?" I say.

Pops's eyes dart around as he furtively pulls me toward the garage. "Now that you're thirteen—"

"Twelve."

He squints. "What's that on your head?"

"That's my camera, remember?" I answer. "I'm a filmmaker."

"You're a what?!"

"I film everything. This ongoing piece is my opus. It's called *A Life So Far*. It's *cinéma vérité*. The truth of real life. It's my signature filmmaking style."

"Hmm." Pop scrunches up his face. "You're a stylist now? You do ladies' hair? I thought you liked to take pictures. Ech, you kids jump from one thing to another."

"No, Pops," I said. "*Cinéma vérité* is my style."

"I don't care what cinema you work at. Take that camera off your head."

I sigh and slide the headpiece off.

He moves in close, his breath smelling a little like garlic-filled socks. "When I was a secret agent in the big war"—he lowers his voice—"I sent messages tied to the legs of pigeons. It's important you know that." He winks.

I don't know what he means, but Pops likes to talk about World War II—how he served in the army, rode around in a rugged jeep, surveyed the bleak countryside, and saw both terrible and sad people. And he especially likes to share stories about his favorite buddies: Joe, Singing Sal, and George. He also likes to talk about my grandma, who was a Lithuanian war bride. He said she loved him because he always told her that he was a lover, not a fighter. I never heard her say that. Mostly she muttered at him in Yiddish or just called him *meshuggana*.

"Now, what I'm going to tell you might sound a little odd," Pops says, tapping his fingers to his head. "And I know what you're thinking. That old Liplock Field isn't as sharp as he used to be. But Ned—"

"Noah."

"Sometimes it's like people aren't listening," he says, shaking his head sadly.

"Is this about you losing your phone again?" I say.

"Haven't you understood a word I've said?" he asks, exasperated.

"Not really."

"Excuse me." Simon comes up behind us. "I have to go."

"You're leaving?" I say, feeling deflated. "So soon? But me and the others were gonna watch KAC."

"KAC?"

"Kids Are Cool. It's the latest kids' indie film festival. Awesome short films made by kids around the world. It's a seventeen-hour marathon. We could watch half tonight and half tomorrow."

"Well, as exciting as that sounds," Simon remarks flatly, "I really do have to go."

"Who are you?" Pops asks, narrowing his eyes at him.

"This is Simon," I introduce him. "Simon, this is my grandfather. We call him Pops."

"Nice meeting you." Simon smiles, then turns to go.

"This is one of your friends?" Pops asks.

"Yes."

"No." Simon and I overlap each other.

"Are all your friends hippies?" Pops asks, scrutinizing Simon.

"Hippies?" Simon, in his straight dark-wash jeans, fitted T-shirt and neat short hair, stares at Pops in disbelief.

"Huh?" I say.

Pops gestures to Simon's chest. There's a faded peace sign on his graphic tee.

"That's just a design, Pops," I say. "It doesn't mean—"

"I liked the color," Simon adds.

"Hmph," Pops remarks, now squinting into his face. "Matches his baby blues. A hippie if ever I've seen one."

Confused, we ponder this for a moment until Simon's like, "Your grandfather . . . I see the similarities. Have a nice day." He turns to go.

"No, no, wait," Pops insists.

He grabs Simon with one hand and me with the other and pulls us into the garage, where he starts rummaging through all these boxes, tossing cellophane wrapping, old newspapers, and all kinds of junk every which way.

"Excuse me, Mr. Noah's Grandfather . . ." Simon starts.

"Call me Pops," Pops says, his head deep in a box, his voice muffled. "Dagnabbit. Just wait one minute . . ." And to himself: "We can stop it. Yes, we can do it. But we're running out of time . . ."

"Pops," I say, "why don't we go back to the party?"

"AHA!" Pop shrieks, making us jump. "Help me out, boys."

We each grab one of his arms and yank. Clutching an envelope tightly in his hand, Pops excitedly waves his fist in the air. Then, much to my surprise, he gets all teary. Simon catches my eye. And I'm wondering, what can this mean?

"You're a good boy, Noah," Pops sniffs, swiping roughly at his glistening eyes. "And not as weird as people think. This is the right time for you."

"Er . . . thanks?" I say uncertainly.

"And you seem like a nice kid too, Saul."

"Simon."

Pops gently extracts a wrinkled yellow paper from the old envelope and unfolds it. He reads the contents, shakes his head, and looks sad. Simon and I peer in, but it's just a page full of dots, marks, and squiggles in faded blue ink.

"What is this?" I ask.

"It's a map," Pops whispers.

"But what does it say?"

Pops sways in close to us and draws out his words slowly. "It says: Dot, dot, dot . . . DOT, dot, squiggle, dot DOT, slash, slash, long line, short line, dot, dot, DOT . . ."

Simon and I wait for a better explanation.

"And that's all I'm sayin'!" Pops says, throwing his scrawny arms in the air.

"Going now," Simon remarks, pivoting on his heel.

"Wait!" Pop shouts. "You don't understand."

"That is an understatement, Mr. Pops," Simon says.

"Here's the thing." Pops grabs Simon by his shoulders and glares into his face. "It's up to you, my grandson . . ."

"Over here, Pops," I say, raising my finger in the air and moving into his line of sight. "I'm your grandson."

"Oh. I know it's you, dagnabbit," Pop grumbles. "I was just trying to include the hippie." He drops his grip on Simon and grabs my shoulders hard. "Up to you. My only grandson . . ."

"You have four other grandsons by Uncle Larry."

"Up to you to save the world!"

Simon examines the map. "It looks like . . . space?" he says.

"Of course it's space! What am I talking about?!"

"We don't really kn—" I start.

"Ach!" Pops exclaims in disgust, folds up the map, puts it back in the envelope, and shoves it deep into the front chest pocket of his baggy button-down shirt. He shuffles past us and heads toward the garage door.

At that moment, a long black car pulls into the driveway and idles there.

"There's my Uber," Pops announces and grabs a suitcase sitting in the corner.

"Wait," I yell after him. "That's it? You haven't explained anything. Where are you going?"

"Fort Lauderdale," he answers.

"Now?"

"Your Aunt Phyllis is waiting for me to open the condo," he says.

"But what about saving the world?" I ask, because now I'm really curious.

"I'll get back to you," he says. "Soon."

And with that he pulls a pair of black sunglasses from his baggy brown pants pocket, puts them on, and climbs into the car. Before it roars off, he leans out the window.

"Don't go anywhere!" he says.

"But," I call out after him, "I'm going to the David Lynch Film Camp!"

CAMP CHALLAH

CHAPTER 3

"I'm *not* going to David Lynch Film Camp?!"

Dad takes my arm and ushers me into the kitchen.

"Sit down, Noah," Mom says, sitting down next to me, her expression serious. A bad sign. Dad plants himself way over by the sink. Also bad.

"There's been a change of plans." Mom places a shiny accordion brochure on the table. "We know you had your heart set on that film camp, but Dad and I agree that this is the right camp for you."

I pick up the brochure. "Camp Challah?" I ask. "But why Camp Challah?"

Mom points to the caption under a cartoon of a crusty round challah with stick figures dancing around it. "Because, see how the strands of the challah bread look like arms? They symbolize brotherhood, truth, peace, and justice. Isn't that nice?"

Now I'm getting a Hebrew school lesson? "I don't mean why is it *called* Camp Challah," I say, exasperated. "I mean I don't want to go to Camp Challah. I want to go to the David Lynch Film Camp."

"But Camp Challah will be fun," Mom says, with a look that's half-forced excitement and half pleading.

"I don't think so." I frown.

"But there are so many activities," Mom gushes. "There's volleyball and canoeing and crafts and campfires with Shabbat sing-alongs . . ."

"Sing-alongs?" I shake my head. "That doesn't sound like me. That sounds—"

Lily swings into the room. "Like preschool? Uh, yeah."

"Maybe camp is the wrong word," Mom says, straining. "It's more like, um, a pre-college program."

"But I'm only in middle school," I say.

"They also offer science, English, current events . . . Oh and here's a course in Israeli dancing. That looks fun," Mom continues, spreading the accordion brochure out wide, pointing to different pictures and captions. "And right across the lake is a historic site where kids can participate in archaeological digs. That sounds fascinating, doesn't it?"

"Yeah, sounds like your jam, Noah," Lily snorts. She fishes an apple from the fridge, takes a crunchy bite and wipes the juice from her chin with the back of her hand. "Just like sixth grade social studies."

"You're going, too," Dad says, swiping her apple and biting into it.

"What?!" Lily spins around. "Excuse me, but no way."

"Yeah, way." Dad chews noisily.

"But what about my friends?" she pleads. "My plans. Going to the beach. And what about the end of summer concert in Jersey? Jules and I have been planning that, like, all year."

"First of all," Dad says, "getting a tan is not a plan and second of all, that overnight thing to Jersey with Jules and Co. was never gonna happen."

"Look, here's something pretty cool." Mom points to another tiny picture in the brochure. "They even have a filmmaking class. Just like filmmaking camp."

"That says camera club, and it's a kid taking a selfie." I grimace, yanking my DLFC brochure from my pocket and unfolding it. "You think this is the same thing as David Lynch Film Camp? See?" I tap aggressively with my pointer finger.

It's plastered with pictures of famous filmmakers and kids holding camera equipment with testimonials. "This says: 'Best summer ever!' And 'The coolest thing in my life!' And 'My screenplay won me an agent!'"

Mom looks to dad for backup.

"Noah," Dad says. "Filmmaking camp is just not realistic for you at this point."

"Why not?"

"It's all the way in Los Angeles for one thing," Mom sighs. "LA is a big city. And there's not much supervision. You'd be on your own a lot. And it's very expensive."

"But it's worth it," I try.

"Besides," Mom continues, like she didn't even hear me, "Rabbi Blum runs Camp Challah and he says it will be a fabulous, fun summer experience."

"Ooh, the rabbi says his camp will be fabulous," says Lily sarcastically, rolling her eyes. "Hold me back!"

"Lily." Dad shuts her down.

"Plus," says Mom, "you just turned twelve, Noah, and it won't be long before your Bar Mitzvah."

"So?" I say.

"Well, it might be a good opportunity to start thinking about a Bar Mitzvah project. There's plenty to choose from at Camp Challah. And Rabbi Blum can help you. You could find something creative."

"How about being a filmmaker?" I offer. "That's creative. At the David Lynch Film Camp, I can make a film about something Jewish or about being Jewish or about Jewish people doing something Jewish or about Jewish studies or about . . ."

"We get it," Dad interrupts, throwing his hands up.

"You do?" I brighten.

"Not really," he says, biting down hard into what's left of his apple.

Mom softens. "What Dad means is that we think Camp Challah is the place for you this summer. Maybe you can go to film camp next summer. You can save up, and you'll be more mature. More . . . aware . . ."

"We hope," Dad mutters.

This is terrible! Beyond terrible. Now I know why they waited so long to tell me. But then it hits me—they just left me an opening. When parents promise something in the future, they're hoping you'll change your mind or forget.

"Really?" I narrow my eyes at Mom. "Next summer? Is that a promise?"

"Um . . . sure." Mom flits her eyes up to dad.

"Can you enunciate that promise clearly into my viewfinder so I can record it?" I ask, tilting my head toward her.

"See, now, this is the problem, Debbie." Dad strides over and tries to yank the headpiece off my head. "Take this camera off!"

"Um—ouch—my hair is caught—"

"Why do you encourage this?" he asks Mom.

"I said *ouch*," I croak, struggling to keep my ears attached.

"Stop! You'll hurt him!" Mom jumps up and jams the camera back on so that now it's down around my mouth.

"Argh!" I say all muffled.

"Hurt him?" Dad tugs at the bands again. "Don't you think this filmmaking fantasy is hurting him?"

"Around my neck—choking!" I whisper hoarsely.

"He's expressing himself. He's an artist," Mom says, yanking the band back over my ears. "And if you don't like that, why don't you play baseball with him or something?"

"Baseball?" Dad booms. "Are we talking about the same kid? The problem is he doesn't have any friends."

"I heard that," I say, finally jerking away.

"There's that new boy, Simon," Mom says. "I was just talking to his mother about . . . you know . . ."

"I don't think I want to go to Camp Challah," I interrupt. "Besides, Pops told me not to go anywhere. He says I'm gonna—"

"What?" Mom snaps, her mom-dar on high alert. "What did Pops say exactly?"

"Nothing," I lie, realizing it's probably better not to mention Pops's wacky stories now.

Mom crosses her arms and arches an eyebrow, with that *I'm waiting for an answer* look, until, suddenly, we hear:

Thump, thump, thump, followed by a sharp yell, coming from outside.

We rush out.

Uncle Larry is sitting at the bottom of the front steps in a heap of wet leaves. Rabbi Blum is crouched beside him, speaking in a comforting tone and holding on to his elbow.

The loud wail of an ambulance siren careens up the block toward us.

"Noah!" Dad yells. "You didn't rake those leaves like I asked you to, and Uncle Larry just fell down the steps. And who the heck called an ambulance?!"

"Um yeah. Sorry. That's a thing," Dr. Marchant

says, gesturing toward Pops's friends from Shady Pines. "They all have smartphones now. And they take videos for Instagram."

"You are so busted!" Lily smirks at me.

While Dr. Marchant helps Uncle Larry into the ambulance, Dad gets up in my face.

"Noah," he says, like he's trying hard to hold his temper, "you need to learn to interact better with people."

"I have fifteen Facebook friends!" I say.

"I said people. Not virtual reality entities floating in space. This is what I'm talking about." His tone turns kind of sad, and he stares into my eyes in a searching way. "You're missing the point of what I'm saying."

"I'm sorry," I say, although I don't think I am. Fifteen Facebook friends is just the beginning of my networking as a filmmaker.

Dad sighs and gives my shoulder a limp pat. "Maybe at camp, away from home, you'll learn to connect better . . ."

"NOAH!"

At that moment, Simon races toward me, hopping over flower beds, swerving around Mom's deer fencing, breathing hard, and looking really mad about something.

CHAPTER 4

"I am going to kill you!" Simon shouts.

"Huh?"

He waves a brochure in my face so hard it makes a slapping sound. "Your mum talked my mum into sending me to Camp Challah?! What's a challah?!"

"It's a braided bread that symbolizes unity and spirituality."

"I don't care!"

"Well, you asked."

"I was being rhetorical!" Simon snaps. "I wasn't looking for a response. I don't want to go to braided bread camp or any camp."

"I'm sure it's inclusive. For everyone," I say. "You don't need to eat challah to go to camp."

"That's not the point!" Simon throws his hands up in the air.

"But maybe it will be fun and help you fit in," I say. "Since you're, like, the new kid and everything and have an accent and that makes you kind of different. And it's hard to fit in, even if you've been living in the same town your whole life. I know about these things."

"Fitting in is not an issue for me." Simon stares at me hard, then sighs loudly and drops his head down to his chest.

"There are activities at Camp Challah," I say, "and some of them look okay in the brochure . . ."

For some reason, I'm now talking Simon into a camp I don't want to go to. Go figure.

"This isn't about your camp," Simon sighs. "Really. It's just that I'm trying to talk my mum and dad into letting me go back to London for the summer. I want to see my mates."

At that moment, a pigeon circles around our heads, cawing loudly.

"They won't let you?" I ask.

"No," Simon says. "They want me to make new mates here."

"That makes sense." I nod.

"Eek, eek, eek!" the pigeon screams as it weaves through the low branches of the trees.

"Makes sense to them." Simon shrugs. "They have

friends here, so what do they care? They just . . . care about themselves sometimes. Know what I mean?"

I wonder if he's being rhetorical again. "Parents are weird," I finally say.

He snorts a laugh, so I'm guessing it was the right thing to say.

"Here." I hand him the Camp Challah brochure. "They have pre-college stuff."

"Do *you* want to go?" He eyes me skeptically.

"No, I want to go to the David Lynch Film Camp in Los Angeles."

Simon opens the accordion pamphlet. "This looks dumb."

"Yeah," I agree.

In the distance, the sky is turning a blue-pink-gray, and the sun is setting behind our neighbors' shingled roofs. The pigeon keeps circling the house until, without warning, it lands right on the camera on my head.

"*Coo!*" he murmurs, spreading his wings.

"What the . . ." Simon jumps back.

"Shoo, shoo." I shake my head in the hopes of dislodging him from his perch.

"*Coo, coo!*" the pigeon responds, except he doesn't fly off. I feel him hopping and dancing around through my hair.

"Get lost!" Simon swipes at him.

The pigeon hops down onto my shoulder.

"What's it doing?" I ask.

"Wait, don't move," says Simon. "There's something tied around his foot. It looks like . . . a little piece of paper."

Carefully I reach up and lift the pigeon off my shoulder. He coos and vibrates in the cup of my hands.

"Shh, shh," I murmur.

"Where did he come from?" Simon asks.

I'm pretty sure I have an idea. I untie the small paper from his leg. He hops back onto my shoulder and poops white and green knotty strands all over my sleeve.

"Gross." Simon scrunches up his face.

"Coo!" the pigeon shouts, then flies away into the watercolor sky.

I unfold the little note. It's covered in shaky, tiny writing in smudged blue ink.

"It's a message from Pops!" I exclaim.

"For real?" Simon looks astonished. "That's mad. That's . . ."

"Pops," I finish his sentence.

The note says: *Get ready to save the world.*

CHAPTER 5

The camp bus screeches to the corner sounding like a giant pterodactyl, its doors yawning open like jaws ready to swallow us up.

The bad news is that I'm saying goodbye to David Lynch Film Camp for now. But the good news is that their website mentions a special end-of-summer two-week session. This is an advanced, invitation-only seminar based on a short film submission. Plus they offer financial aid.

So I figure if I if I do a good job participating at Camp Challah, make some friends, and make a great, *short* opus, I can score an invitation and convince mom and dad to let me go.

While other kids say quick goodbyes to their parents and start filing onto the bus, Mom gives Lily and me happy bon voyage hugs. I overhear Dad giving Lily the talk about having a good attitude.

". . . Keep an eye on . . . Noah . . . blah, blah, blah . . . Noah . . ." he says, speaking really low.

Lily makes a gaggy sound at the back of her throat and rolls her eyes.

"Have fun!" Mom sings, looking all nervous like she's afraid I might not.

Dad pats me on the back. "Yeah, have fun and . . . Noah, for God's sake, try to read the room."

Simon is standing nearby with his parents. They're what my mom would call a handsome couple, and they have super good posture. Plus their clothes seem pretty fancy for saying goodbye at the bus stop.

Simon's dad calls him "son" a lot, and they're saying something about rallying, giving it his all, and making American friends.

The minute they're back in their car, Simon goes back to brooding and sweeping through his phone, probably looking at pictures of his mates. As for me, I've rolled up the brochure to the DLFC and shoved it into one of my socks.

"Gettin' in?" grunts the bus driver in a way that seems more like telling than asking.

I grab my camera headpiece from my backpack, secure it around my head, and step up into the bus.

"Hey," Lily whispers sharply from behind. "Take that thing off. Now."

"But I'm filming my short opus for the DLFC extended summer program," I whisper back.

"Well, you look freaky," she answers.

"Actually, he looks like a guy who does construction on the highway at night," Simon remarks, climbing up the steps behind us.

"And that's better?" she says.

"Well, maybe not," he says, flashing a toothy white smile. "Don't think we've formally met. I'm Simon. From *London*." He says that last part like it's super important.

"Uh huh." Lily looks down at her phone and slides past me down the aisle.

"Well, that went well," Simon mumbles.

"Don't take it personally," I say. "She's not friendly—unless you're popular."

"Maybe I should be popular," Simon says softly, his eyes sliding toward her.

"She's also mad because she doesn't want to go to camp either," I say.

As I make my way down the aisle, kids glance up, then look down. I get that a lot. It's like, "Oh, it's just you. Not interested."

My stomach wobbles, and I wipe my clammy hands down the front of my T-shirt.

"Sit down, Noah." Simon nudges me gently from behind.

"Sit down!" echoes the bus driver, lifting one sharply outlined orange eyebrow.

The doors shut, and the bus jerks forward.

"Grab a seat," Simon urges me again.

Right away, Lily's cool-dar connects with some cute girls sitting toward the back. She catches their eyes. They smile and slide over. And, bam, she's in.

How does she do that?

Moving forward, I nervously scan for a place, but every kid with a window seat throws a backpack on the open seat in rhythm. Slam, Slam, Slam.

I'm closing in on the back. Not good. That's usually where the mean kids sit.

Two big guys with short necks, looking like they already shave, sneer at me. They're like a pair of unfriendly Rottweilers behind a chain-link fence, tethered together at the neck, watching their next meal approach.

"Do you have guys like that in London?" I whisper over my shoulder to Simon.

"Yeah. Best to sit anywhere soon," he warns,

and with that, someone makes room for him, and he slides into a now-empty seat.

"Sit down *now!*" the bus driver barks, not even glancing in her rearview mirror. I wonder if she has some kind of bionic sensors under her beehive hair.

"Hey, you! What's that on your head?" one of the big Rottweilers says. "Are you a roach exterminator or something?"

Kids laugh. Lily glares at me.

"Yeah, sit down, roach guy," the other one says, making them both guffaw.

Suddenly, the bus jolts to a stop, and I fall forward. I try to grab one of the seat handles, but my already sweaty hands—now super sweaty—slide off the metal bar, and I stumble right into the bigger Rottweiler's lap.

The bus explodes in laughter.

I squirm to right myself, but between the narrow seat and the weight of my backpack, I'm wedged in tight.

"Get off!" he yells, pushing me hard.

But I can only roll and squirm, roll and squirm.

"Sorry, sorry, sorry," I mumble, my face squashed against his chest. The other Rottweiler is giggling hysterically at a surprisingly high pitch.

Finally, between his shoving and my squirming, I'm on my feet.

"Sorry. My backpack got me stuck. It's like being a turtle."

Somewhere I think I hear Simon groan. Maybe that wasn't the right thing to say.

"Hey Mike, you got a turtle friend," the other Rottweiler giggles. "A little turtle friend sitting in your lap."

"Shut up, Jake!" he snaps.

A white-hot burn crawls up my cheeks, and the loud muffled roar of kids sounds like a beach seashell at my ear.

But they're not just laughing at me. Rottweiler Mike's face flushes bright red too. He grabs a handful of my shirt, bumping my headpiece askew, and glares into my eyes.

"Listen, Turtle," he says, and his breath smells like he just ate a whole pizza with extra garlic. "We've been coming to this camp for four years. Now, I don't wanna be mean or anything . . ."

He doesn't want to be mean?!

"'Cause I'm not a bad guy," Mike declares. "But I can tell already that you're the kind of kid who messes stuff up. Maybe not even on purpose. Maybe you don't even know you're, like, in the way or causin' problems or anything."

This conversation is turning into one of those talks I have with the school counselor.

"But I got stuff to do this summer," he says. "Business to attend to. And I need to do it right. To concentrate."

He needs to concentrate on business? At camp?

"So you stay out of my way, and I'll stay out of yours," he says. "But mess me up, and I'm gonna mess you up."

"'Kay," I squeak, feeling like I'm gonna pass out from the fumes of his breath.

I have no idea what he's talking about but, fortunately, the bus grinds to a stop, and more kids get on, breaking the tension. Mike releases me with a shove.

I'm feeling kind of weird, like totally lost, and my stomach is starting to hurt. These camp kids are tough, and I haven't even gotten to camp yet.

Suddenly, a gray backpack decorated with about a million pins creeps over an empty seat. Then, bam, it's on the floor. Someone is making room for me!

I throw myself into the vacated seat.

"Thanks!" I beam at the girl sitting by the window.

She stares at me over the top of her book then brushes away a frizzy tendril of brown hair that's escaped from one of her two long braids. She seems like someone who likes nature, in her green-beige T-shirt that looks like it's been washed too many times, tan cargo shorts, and scuffed-up brown hiking boots.

And there's a row of small earrings crawling up around the side of each ear. They're cartilage piercings, and I know this because a few months ago, Lily wanted cartilage piercings but Dad was like, "That's not happening."

"For making room, I mean," I add.

She lifts her book up higher.

"Because there was nowhere to sit and you made room."

"Yeah." She shifts her body toward the window.

"'Cause I was standing and had nowhere to sit. And I think that guy in the back is super mad at me. Doesn't he look like a Rottweiler?"

She makes a very loud sighing noise, shifts her whole body toward the window, and lifts the book up so that it covers her whole face.

"Hi," I say, leaning toward her. "Watcha reading?"

She holds the book up for me to see.

"*Plastics: The Silent Killer*," I read aloud. "Is that science fiction? My sister Lily used to love to read about hot supernatural guys. Now she likes to read about time travel."

"It's about the environment," she says flatly. "How people are destroying the planet with plastic so they can keep their veggies in containers that burp."

"Containers that burp?"

"Like when you close them and make them airtight?" she says, like it's a question. Then she raises an eyebrow like she's pretty sure I don't get it, which I don't.

Sighing and looking exasperated, she turns toward me and points to her oversized T-shirt.

"Um . . . nice shirt," I say uncertainly.

"No, this," she emphatically jabs her chest with her finger.

I lean in and read the faded words: *Earth is Dying.*

"Ah. Gotcha." I nod like I understand, but I have so many questions I want to ask her.

I want to know why Earth is dying. Is it only because of plastic burping containers or other things? And how long does it have to live? Does she know for a fact that it's dying, or does she just think so?

Will we have any warning? Or will it just be dead one morning? And how will we know?

I'm just about to launch into a bunch of questions when I remember what Dad said about reading people's faces. Her face looks like it wants to bite me.

"I'm Noah," I finally say.

"Hey," she grumbles, then places two earbuds in her ears. She turns and gazes out the window, balancing her scruffy work boots up on a black guitar case at her feet. The name *Mia* is written across it in squiggly gold paint. I guess that's her.

We cruise onto the highway. After a while, everyone sways into the ride, listens to music, or plays on their phones. It seems pretty clear that Mia is engrossed in her dead Earth book, so I pull out my phone to upload my latest film footage, when I hear a voice mumbling low.

"Huh? Are you talking to me, Mia?" I turn to her. "I hope you're not mad, Mia, that I guessed your name's Mia, but it's on your guitar case, unless it's someone else's guitar case, but why would a girl who's not Mia have a case with the name Mia on it and . . ."

From the bottom of her throat comes this weird growly vibrating sound, and it grows stronger until it's just the right volume.

And I realize she's not talking to me at all.

She's singing softly, a tuneless kind of song that starts out with mumbles and grows into formed words. Some of the verses are awkward rhymes, and the chorus is something about recycling, the crying earth, mangled plastics, lady times of the month and lunar cycles, her Bat Mitzvah, and starting a new chapter in her life.

And she does this all the way to Camp Challah.

CHAPTER 6

Finally, we arrive!

The bus squeals to a halt. Mia grabs her backpack and stands. "S'cuse me," she says tightly.

I try and twist my feet out of the way, but she steps all over them anyway.

"Bye!" I wave. "See you at camp!"

"Yeah . . . probably not," she says, without looking back, and shuffles up the aisle.

"Watch yer step!" the bus driver barks, in a way that sounds like she wants us to hurry up and doesn't care if we watch our steps or not.

The Rottweilers push their way off, while the rest of us collect our stuff and head for the door, onto the grass and into a bright, warm day.

"Long ride, eh?" Simon moans and stretches.

There's so much to see!

The first thing I notice is the tall signpost with skinny arrows indicating where things are, like the mess hall, the baseball field, the lake, the outhouses, the girls' bunks, and the boys' bunks. And there's a long arrow-shaped sign, pointing to a path that looks like it winds beyond the lake. It reads, *Levy Homestead Historic Site.*

"Shalom!" Rabbi Blum exclaims.

He and Mrs. Blum are standing by the flagpole, greeting all the campers they can grab. Mrs. Blum is sharing happy shoulder squeezes. Rabbi Blum is heartily giving everyone high-fives with one hand while sipping from a huge metallic coffee mug with the other.

He usually dresses like other middle-aged guys like my dad and Principal Lefrak, but for camp he's gone all hipster in his denim yarmulke, mustard cargo pants, and graphic T-shirt imprinted with the challah and dancing figures from the brochure.

"Whaz up?! Whaz up?!" he shouts exuberantly, his grin showing through his stubbly beard.

"Shalom," "Yeah, hi," "What's up?" the kids mumble as they pass down the greeting line.

"Noah!" He takes my arm and pulls me into his face. "Now, I want you to have a good summer."

"Um, okay," I mutter uncertainly.

"And don't worry so much about things," he says, all serious.

"Er, okay," I say, trying to gently pull away.

"Your dad tells me you're worried about making friends," he speaks low and confidentially.

"Well, not rea—" I start.

"And your mom says," he interrupts, "you're worried about your Bar Mitzvah project."

"Well, no, I don't really care righ—"

"Mom also says you like to make movies. And I just want you to know that that's not weird. You're not weird."

"I'm not?"

"Not at all. Everyone loves watching movies. Mrs. Blum and I love watching movies."

"Okay."

"Now, you know my son, Nathan, yes?" He brightens, gesturing to Nathan, milling awkwardly in a group of happy, chatting counselors.

"Sure." I nod.

Nathan looks like a skinnier, less peppy version of the rabbi. He nods in a shy, aimless way at people, then pulls a paperback book from the pocket of his brown cargo pants and starts reading.

"Nathan!" the Rabbi calls over to him disapprovingly. "Put the book down," he mouths, motioning with his mug.

Nathan startles and shoves the paperback into one of his over-crammed pockets.

"He's in high school now, so he's a counselor this summer," the Rabbi continues. "He's gonna help you eleven-and-ups with your Bar and Bat Mitzvah projects. That'll be fun, right?!"

Not really. "Sure," I mumble, as he finally releases me in order to latch on to the next kid.

Groan. There's got to be some good hiding places here in the woods.

After the greeting line, we're bounced over to the counselors to get our introductory packets and color-coded bunk tags. I'm happy to see that Simon and I are in the red bunk.

"Hey." Nathan extends a limp, clammy hand to me and then to Simon. "So I'm your counselor," he says, his eyes darting to our faces then traveling over our heads.

"Looks like it," Simon agrees affably.

"Soooo . . . yeah." Nathan looks like he might have cramps. He glances at the pocket where his book peeks out the top, like he can't wait to get back to it.

All around us, kids are connecting with their bunkmates and their counselors, who mostly look pretty cool and welcoming. Lily's counselor's name tag reads "Janine." She's smiley and has pretty teeth and looks like an older version of Lily. Lily and her new friends from the bus shriek when they realize they're all in the same bunk. Janine points them toward the girls' cabins, and they chat excitedly on their way there.

"Um, should we . . . go somewhere?" I ask Nathan.

"Oh right, right," he replies, digging into one of his empty pockets. "We're Bunk 4, but first let me give you your badges—wait, they're here somewhere . . . was looking for that pen," he mumbles. "These tissues are gross . . . ticket stub from Shavuot . . . hang on . . ."

Finally, he extracts a pack of crumpled, torn, colored badges. It's kind of like a magician pulling a long string of colorful handkerchiefs from up his sleeve. "Here you go! They have stick backs, so you can wear them if you want."

"I'm good," Simon says, shoving his into his pocket.

Nathan presses one to his shirt, and it quickly slides off. He fumbles, trying to stick it on again, and it slides again. And it seems like this might go on for a while.

"So, we'll see you later, then, Nathan," Simon says.

"Bunk 4!" Nathan waves to us as we weave into the traveling clusters of kids.

"Whew, that was painful," Simon remarks, then tilts his head back into his phone. "Yes! Wi-Fi! At least we're still in civilization."

Passing the Rottweilers, I hear Mike say, "Another summer, more to find." He fist bumps Jake. I'm wondering what that means when one of them shoves me, knocking me off balance.

"Watch it, Turtle," Mike grunts.

"Just ignore them," Simon says.

Lily brushes past me, laughing with her pack of girls, barely glancing my way. I'm guessing she'll spend the whole summer pretending we're not related.

"Thank God we don't look alike," she said to me once. That kind of hurt my feelings, but Mom says some siblings don't get along their whole lives until their parents die.

That made me feel even worse—and also kind of nervous. I hope that one day Lily and I can be friends before someone I love drops dead.

Simon glances up and stares as she scuttles off

with her new besties, his face all slack and dreamy. She must feel his eyes on her because she glances his way and tosses him a smile. Even I can tell he's got a big crush. Oh well. When she rejects him, he can't say I didn't try to warn him.

In the distance, a blue lake shimmers under a colorful, wispy, pink-and-gray sky, and beyond that is a stretch of woods. The air smells sweet and pine-scented.

I spot Mia, walking with some girls who are probably her bunkmates. They're talking excitedly. Mia leans in, nods, and trots to keep up.

Simon and I reach the grassy clearing where Bunk 4 awaits.

Inside the cabin is rustic, like a class trip to a pioneer village. There are a few bureaus, two sets of bunkbeds, and two nice-size windows—one offering a view of the signpost path and, beyond that, the lake.

"It'll have to do, eh?" Simon says and throws his stuff onto a bed to claim it.

Within minutes, our bunkmates arrive, and we all exchange "heys" and introduce ourselves.

"Nathan sent us here," says the one named Tyler. He's skinny with brown hair and glasses.

"He's kinda weird," the other one, named Josh, adds with a grin. He's dark and sporty-looking with reddish brown hair.

We quickly learn that they're friends. They like Simon's accent and both have even been to London. Simon's excited to show them his phone pics of his mates playing soccer, which he says is called football in London.

They want to know about the camera on my head, so I tell them about my opus and the DLFC extended summer program. They take turns making faces into my viewfinder and want to know if they're going to be famous on YouTube. I tell them you never know.

"What's an opus?" Tyler asks.

"It's the story of my life so far," I say. "So I call it *A Life So Far*. I'm interested in *cinéma vérité*. That's a French term which means—"

"That's cool, Nick," Josh interrupts, his eyes sliding away from me.

"Noah," I correct him, adjusting my camera headpiece.

"There are some hot girls here," Josh says, grabbing a ball from his duffel and tossing it up and down. "Whaddaya think?"

"I talked to a girl on the bus," I say. "She was cool and sang in a growly way in the back of her throat."

Josh stops tossing and everyone turns to stare at me.

"Did you guys see her?" I ask.

"Um . . . sure," Tyler says, but he doesn't look sure. "Hey, Simon, want to throw a ball around before dinner?"

"Yeah," Simon replies, as Josh tosses the ball to Tyler, and they laugh and shove each other out of the bunk.

He starts after them, but I'm not sure what to do. They didn't ask me. My stomach drops a little.

"Come on," says Simon.

"Um . . . I'm okay," I say.

"Right then." Simon heads toward the door but stops in his tracks. He pulls his fingers through his hair, hesitates, then turns back.

"Come on, Noah," he coaxes.

"S'all right," I say, turning toward my duffel. I should unpack. Because, like Mom says, my stuff won't unpack itself.

"Should I put my shirts in with my shorts, or should I have a drawer for each? It looks like there are only five drawers, so that means one drawer each. And what about my underwear? Should the socks be somewhere else? And what about the dirty stuff? Where's the blue laundry bag Mom packed? And where can I put my computer so it won't be exposed to moisture?"

"Come on, Noah," Simon repeats, taking the shirt I'm holding and tossing it onto the bed.

"But . . . what if they play with the Rottweilers?"

"Who?"

"Mike and Jake," I say quietly, even though there's no one around.

"Don't fret about it." Simon grabs my arm. "But, um, how about you take the camera off your head first?"

"I dunno . . ." I hesitate.

"OW!" I bark as he yanks it off.

"Sorry, not sorry," he says dryly, clamping on to my arm. "Now let's go."

CHAPTER 7

We toss the ball around for a while (I'm mostly chasing it) until it's time for dinner. The mess hall is a crowded, noisy, cavernous place that has what my chorus teacher, Mr. Glutz, calls "good acoustics." Voices swirl up into the air and reverberate, sounding like one dull thumping noise. The pigeons nesting in the rafters make vibrating cooing sounds. I wonder if any of them knows Pops.

Simon, Josh, Tyler, and I line up for food, which is hamburgers, fries, and carrot sticks. I scan the long tables and benches for the Rottweilers and spot them by the window, eating with a bunch of guys who also drool while they eat and have dopey laughs.

Not far from them, the counselors look like they're splitting up into cool and not-so-cool cliques. Janine leads the happily chatting main clique, while a few hangers-on sit nearby, lean in, and nod. Nathan sits a few seats away and doesn't seem that interested in whether he's included or not. He munches on fries, his head down in his book.

We amble to the other side of the room.

"Why do they have to ruin a perfectly good meal with stuff that's good for you?" Josh remarks. "I hate freakin' carrot sticks."

"And if you move them around the plate like this in a little frizzy pile, they look like your hair, Josh," I say.

"Say that again"—Josh picks up a carrot stick and waves it at me—"and I'll have to kill you."

"What?!"

"He's kidding, Noah," Simon says. "Lighten up. Don't be so literal."

"Hey," says a familiar voice from behind.

It's Lily and her friends.

Simon brightens. "Oh hi, Lily."

Josh and Tyler catch eyes and snicker. Tyler makes a quiet kissing noise, and Simon gives Tyler a kick.

"Care to join us?" Simon asks her, gesturing to a nearby spot on the bench.

"Oh, yes, please do join us," Tyler imitates Simon's fancy accent.

"And bring the Queen," Josh adds.

They guffaw and shove fries into their mouths. Simon kicks Tyler again.

"Cut it out!" Tyler says, spraying everyone with bits of fries.

"You cut it out!" Simon throws a carrot stick at him, but it lands on Josh's head and looks totally like his natural hair, proving my point.

Lily's friends make clucking noises with their tongues and roll their eyes.

"Well, as fun as this seems," Lily says sarcastically, "we'll sit at this end of the table. I just came by to check on Noah."

"Really?" I say, because this surprises me a lot. "But you never check on me. I think you came over to see Simon."

"Whooaa!" Tyler and Josh explode, then double over laughing.

"NO-AH," Lily says in a clipped, annoyed way, bugging her eyes out at me. "You're so . . . disconnected." She makes a disgusted noise, but I can see she's blushing.

"Actually, I'm not disconnected," I say. "I said that on purpose to embarrass you."

This makes Tyler and Josh really crack up.

"You're okay, Noah," Tyler says and Josh nods.

Suddenly there's the loud clinking sound of a fork against an aluminum travel coffee mug.

"Hello! Hello! Can I have your attention?" Rabbi Blum shouts. "I want you all to meet your head counselor and camp leader, Yipsy Green-baum. I think you'll also find him to be a good friend."

"Hey everyone!" Yipsy exclaims.

"What kind of a name is Yipsy?" Simon whispers.

"And this is my old friend Mick Jagger," Yipsy says, referring to a small, wiry hairball of a dog. "Say, hey, Mick," Yipsy instructs him.

Mick Jagger yaps a few times and lies down at Yipsy's feet.

Rabbi Blum's phone rings loudly, filling the room with a full chorus of "Tradition" from *Fiddler on the Roof*. "What do you mean the synagogue's air conditioning system shut down?" he blurts.

Moving briskly toward the door, he waves his cup at Yipsy, like he wants him to take over. "Call my wife . . . She's where?"

"So," Yipsy continues. "Like Rabbi Blum just explained, I'm pretty much the guy in charge."

Yipsy's in charge? He's pretty young, maybe in college. I know this because my cousin's in college, although Yipsy is way hairier than he is, with his dark beard and lots of dark curls. And he's dressed in an old-school tie-dyed shirt and cargo shorts. He's also got super fuzzy legs and wears sandals, like the hiker kind with bands all over them.

"I'll make sure you have fun while your parents are home enjoying the quiet or are out boogieing," he says enthusiastically.

"What's boogieing?" Tyler whispers to us.

"He means dancing," Simon says.

Josh pretends to check his phone. "Oh look, the 1980s called. They want Yipsy back."

Someone makes a loud farting noise.

"Now settle down." Yipsy makes a calming motion, flattening his palms against the air. "Not long ago, I was a camper like you, making the same obnoxious noises, but listen up. We're gonna have a great time this summer."

At this point, a scowling stocky lady strides in, a laptop under her beefy arm and her hair pulled back in a tight bun. She wears purple leggings and a purple velour hoodie with a black bag strapped across her body.

Yipsy gestures to her. "But first, let me introduce this lovely lady here, your mom away from home, Nurse Leibowitz."

"Hello," she says in a baritone voice, narrowing her eyes at us.

Mick Jagger whines and belly-crawls under a nearby table.

"She's nothing like my mom." Josh makes a face.

"Nurse Leibowitz is new to Camp Challah," Yipsy continues, "and I bet she's feeling a little uncertain, maybe a little nervous . . ."

Nurse Leibowitz glares at him sternly.

"Or not," Yipsy mutters. Then to us: "How about we give her a big Camp C hey!"

"Hey," comes the halfhearted response.

Nurse Leibowitz whispers something in Yipsy's ear.

"Seems that Nurse Leibowitz has prepared a short safety video for you."

She pushes a large-screen TV into the middle of the room and connects her computer.

"Great." Tyler rolls his eyes.

We're subjected to five minutes of a really gory self-made YouTube video, with pictures of all the bloody, awful things that can happen at camp if you're not careful, like:

- deadly snake bites
- dismemberment from boating accidents caused by fooling around
- getting lost in the woods and dehydrating to death
- swimming with no lifeguards and drowning

And so on, until we're all super nervous and a few of the younger kids in the back are crying.

"So, you see, children," Nurse Leibowitz says, switching off her computer, "safety before fun."

"Er, thank you," Yipsy says uncomfortably. "That was very informative."

"I could be at the football club right now hanging out with my mates," Simon laments, sadly swiping through his phone.

"Now," says Yipsy with a smile, "here's something really fun . . ."

Nurse Leibowitz scowls at him.

"Um . . . safe and fun. We have lots of traditions at Camp C. We have our awesome Friday night

Shabbat services, accompanied by marshmallow roasts and sing-alongs by the campfire, weather permitting, as well as a whole host of courses and activities, many of which incorporate a Jewish perspective. Now this summer, we're offering three new rockin' courses. First, Israeli folk dancing with Ari, who's visiting from Israel. Let's make him feel at home."

"Hey," "Hi," "Whaz up," "How you doin'," "Charmed I'm sure," we all mumble—that last remark coming from Simon, who responds to our eye rolls with a smirky "What?"

"Second," Yipsy continues, "for you eleven-and-ups, we now have pre-Bar and Bat Mitzvah Project preparation, discussion and idea sharing with Nathan Blum, who's very excited about helping you discover your mitzvah."

I glance at Nathan, slouched over his book, his mouth slightly open, concentrating like nothing else in the world exists. Ari elbows Nathan. His head shoots up, his eyes looking like they're refocusing on reality. He mumbles an anemic "Hey."

"And finally," Yipsy continues, "this is really special. We're starting a new Camp C tradition. Every other night, we're gonna have something called Show Your Stuff."

A loud wolf whistle slides from the direction of the Rottweilers.

"Don't get frisky now," Yipsy chuckles, his shoulders bobbing up and down. "It's an opportunity to display your talent. Like painting or dancing, sharing something you like to do or something you learned here at camp. So if anyone wants to . . ." he cups his hand around his ear.

Silence.

"If you want to . . ." he cups around his ear again. Nothing.

"What's he doing?" I ask.

"I think he's cueing us," Simon says.

"Show. Your. Stuff!" Yipsy shouts. "Let me hear you."

"Show your stuff," a few kids mumble.

"I can't hear you," Yipsy sings.

Simon shakes his head. "He's mental."

"Show your stuff," a few more kids mumble.

"What?!" Yipsy squints. "Come on, I know you can do better than that."

"Ugh, someone put him out of his misery already," Josh says, flopping his head down on the table.

Nurse Leibowitz whispers in his ear.

"Nurse Leibowitz says if someone doesn't volunteer, she's gonna give you all early flu shots." Yipsy forces a laugh. "But she's just kidding, right, Nurse Leibowitz? What a kidder."

Nurse Leibowitz doesn't crack a smile.

"Me," a voice finally rings out.

Yipsy beams. We all shift and pivot to see where the voice is coming from. And from out of a lone seat in the shadows in the corner, Mia stands up.

"I want to sing," she says.

CHAPTER 8

"Who's that?" Lily asks, scrunching up her nose like she's just smelled something bad.

Mia clomps up to the front of the room, the tongues of her boots flapping as she goes. She noisily drags a stool across the floor, climbs onto it, places her guitar across her knees, and stares solemnly out into the faces of the curious, whispering campers.

Excitedly, I fumble for my phone and push *record*.

"What's your name?" Yipsy asks.

"Mia," she responds coolly.

"So, Mia, what are you gonna rock us out to?"

"It's an original song," she announces.

She strums her guitar with one hand, adjusting the knobs of the neck with the other, which makes the chords go all wonky. A few minutes pass, and kids start fidgeting.

"What's she waiting for?" Simon says.

"Isn't she awesome?" I say.

"She's . . . something." Simon frowns.

"Sing, sing, sing!" some kids begin to chant.

Finally, Mia begins, her warbly voice lifting into the eaves.

Out the window behind her, the early evening sky is turning another shade of gray, and the moon is low and full. Its crevices and shadows give the impression of a lopsided, smiling face on a flat white head. It makes a cool background shot for my short opus.

This time, Mia's song is about the trees and rivers turning from green to mucky brown, about animals covered in sludge and dying with glassy eyes, and about the air becoming a wall of thick gray smoke. The last verse is about remembering to recycle, leading to a high note about nuclear waste. She strums another loud chord for emphasis, stops abruptly, and stares deadpan into the crowd.

"Yikes!" Tyler's eyebrows arch into his forehead.

"Well, that was cheery," Josh remarks.

Yipsy smiles, bobs his head up and down, and leads a few scattered claps as Mick Jagger barks and wags his tail.

Looking satisfied—oblivious to the farting noises, snorts, and sneezes of the word "loser"—Mia hops off the stool and returns to her seat, where her bunkmates have their faces buried in their phones.

Chairs scrape as everyone starts for the door.

My friends might think she's strange, but Mia's singing makes me feel tingly and new. Like when you accidentally pick up a dog's shock collar by the electric fence. Or like when waves crash up on the beach and spray cold spikes of water, burning your sunburned skin like fiery pricks. Or like when you stand outside right before a storm and a tree branch whips into your face. Or like when unexpected thunder cracks so hard, you feel your bladder squeeze a little . . .

"Noah? Noah, are you in there?" Simon snaps his fingers in front of my face.

"Huh?"

"Time to go," Josh says.

As my new friends and I file out of the mess hall, I shoot Mia a thumbs up. The corners of her mouth twitch into a smile before she turns away and bumps her chair closer to her bunkmates, who are huddled together, laughing about something.

As we amble across the clearing, Josh finds a

glow Frisbee on the ground, and he and Tyler start whizzing it back and forth.

"I thought she was cool," I say to Simon, who's swiping his phone.

He doesn't answer and he looks kind of somber and I can't tell if he's sad or just concentrating. I want to ask him more questions, like what his friends' names are, what he likes about them, what kinds of things they do together, and if he thinks that we can ever be good friends.

But the only thing I can figure is that he looks like he doesn't want to talk.

Now the sky is inky dark blue. Stars are popping like white pricks through a black cloth, and only the tiki lights along the path and the bright moon light the way. That space between night and day feels like something between different times and worlds. It's like anything magical can happen, and Mia's song loops over and over in my head.

Suddenly, I'm inspired!

"Hey, I have an idea!" I say to Simon. "I'm gonna put the footage of Mia singing into my short audition film for the DLFC extended summer program."

Simon glances up as if he suddenly remembers I'm here. "Is that a good idea?"

"Sure," I answer. "It's perfect. And I can even, like, preview my film—at 'Show Your Stuff!'"

"Noah . . ." he starts, but at that moment, a pigeon swoops down from the trees, circles around over my head, and lands squarely on my shoulder.

"Could that be the same pigeon from before?" Simon asks.

"Must be," I say, blinking back from his flapping wings.

"Hold still," Simon commands. "I've got to get a picture of this for my mates. Smile!"

He shoots and sends it. Within seconds, his phone pings back.

"My mates think your bird friend is brilliant," he laughs. "They say we should give him a name."

"Hmm. A name . . . that's a good idea. How about Sal?" I offer, thinking of Pops's singing buddy from the army.

"Sal." Simon ponders for a moment. "I like it. Hold on now, Sal." Simon gently reaches for the little ragged paper attached to his leg. But Sal keeps hopping out of his reach, turning, dancing down my arm and back again.

"I'll hold him," I say. I reach up, and he hops into my hand, cooing and vibrating as I stroke his chest.

Simon unties the note. We hold our breath in anticipation as I unfold it. "What's it say?" Simon asks.

"It says, *The clock is ticking!* and *Saving the world takes gumption!*"

"What's gumption?"

"It's an old-fashioned word for courage."

"Wait." Simon moves toward Sal, who is still hopping around on my shoulder. "Looks like there's a note on his other leg."

Gently, he reaches in and unties that one. It reads, *Got gumption?*

"What in the ruddy world is he talking about now?" Simon mutters in way that sounds rhetorical.

Do I have gumption? Generally, I think I do. I mean, no one likes to think of themselves as cowardly. But if I were in a dangerous situation, what would I do? Run? Defend myself? Would I have enough gumption to save someone else? Or, in this case, would I have the courage to save the world, which is basically inhabited by a bunch of strangers?

I find the stub of a pencil in my pocket.

I scribble my answer on one of the tiny slips of paper, attach it back to Sal's foot, and shoo him off into the night sky. I feel all tingly with excitement.

The note says, *YES.*

CHAPTER 9

Now we have three notes from Pops. And all this intrigue is making my stomach feel kind of jumpy—but in a good way. We head toward the bunk, and Simon and I are really psyched about sharing the story with Josh and Tyler.

"But first, we've got to get rid of Nathan," Simon announces.

"Why?"

"He's a counselor," Simon says, wrinkling his nose.

"Don't you like him?" I ask.

"That's not the point," Simon replies curtly.

I feel like he thinks I should just know what the point is. I don't.

"I mean, it's not that I don't *like* him," Simon adds. "He just—well, he doesn't have to hang out with us, now does he?"

He explains that he's that heard the counselors don't usually hang out with the campers after dark. Mostly, they just check to see you're okay and then meet up with their friends at the canteen on the other side of the clearing. But Simon's nervous that Nathan doesn't really have any friends. And Simon thinks the only upside of going to sleepaway camp is the chance to be kind of independent and not have someone older breathing down your neck.

Josh and Tyler are already in the cabin, playing games on Josh's computer. Simon puts his finger to his lips, signaling for them to be quiet, and points to the slightly open door between our bunk and Nathan's.

Simon knocks and pokes his head inside. "Hello, Nathan," he says in his cheery, clipped British way.

Nathan is sitting up in bed, reading.

"Just letting you know we're in for the night," Simon says.

"Oh." Nathan glances up. "What time is it?"

"He didn't even know you were gone," Josh mumbles, rolling his eyes.

"Not too late, so not to worry," Simon replies.

"Um, okay," Nathan says and starts butt-hopping towards the end of the bed. "Did you want to, like, talk or something?"

"No, no." Simon holds his palms up. "We're totally fine."

Nathan looks questioningly at me. I nod in confirmation.

"We're just going to hang out. You know . . ." Simon's sentence fades off.

"'Kay." Nathan looks kind of relieved and kind of unsure at the same time.

Outside, several counselors laugh loudly, and I recognize Janine's giggle and flirty banter.

"I'll be here," Nathan says with a wan smile. "With my book," he adds, holding it up—like, just in case we didn't know what he meant. "So . . . 'night. Let me know if you nee—"

"'Night then," Simon interrupts, pushes me back, and quickly closes the door. "Well, let's hope that sets a precedent."

"Whaddaya mean?" I ask.

"He means," says Tyler, "hopefully Nathan'll get the idea that we want to hang out by ourselves."

"Do you think he's, like, lonely?" I ask.

"He's got all the other counselors to hang out with." Josh shrugs disinterestedly, his attention concentrated on his laptop.

Out the window, I see Jake and Sarah from

Bunks 5 and 9 trotting toward Janine & Co.

"You're so slow! Hurry up!" calls Sarah affectionately as she links arms with Cooper from Bunk 2.

They chat and laugh as they head toward the shadowed, needly pine trees and the dim yellow glow of the little canteen beyond.

Next door, I hear Nathan padding around. There's a click, and the white light seeping under the crack of our door shuts off. I'm guessing he's going to bed, even though it's only about nine o'clock.

Eagerly, Simon starts describing what happened with Pops to Tyler and Josh. His excitement gets me excited until we're totally babbling over each other. At first, Josh and Tyler don't believe us, but when Simon shows them the picture of Sal on my shoulder, they're like, "Whooaaaa!"

"Sal's a carrier pigeon," Tyler says. "I've read about those."

They agree that the notes are very mysterious.

"These are from your pops?" Tyler asks, delicately examining them. "That's amazing. He must be really smart or something."

"Mmm . . . or something," Simon says.

Josh shoots him a questioning look.

"No offense, Noah," Simon says, "but your pops

75

is a little . . ." He makes a circling motion with his finger around his ear. "It's possible the notes don't mean anything at all."

"It's hard to know" is all I can think to say, which is how I feel.

Sometimes I think Pops is a little out there, but sometimes I think he's super smart. After all, he knew how to train Sal, and he knew how to be a lover and not a fighter in World War II, and he knew how to survive to be ninety-something years old.

"I have an idea," Tyler says exuberantly.

He writes down all the letters from the notes on a piece of paper, cuts each one out, and spreads them all out on the floor.

"Maybe the notes are anagrams," he says. "That's when the letters stand for different words, and you have to mix them up to figure it out."

When he shuffles the letters around, we actually get some interesting combinations:

Tel her so

Where vat does

Wade over stlh

That last one makes the least sense until Tyler reasons that maybe *stlh* is code for the name Stella, like some sort of double secret code.

At first we're all super revved-up about that idea, batting it around for a while, until we realize that I don't know a Stella and that it's not only a stretch but also kind of dumb. Finally we agree that none of the anagrams make any more sense than just plain "Save the world," which seems pretty clear.

At this point, it's getting super late, and Yipsy pops his head in the door. Mick Jagger rushes over to me, all waggles and wiggles.

"Hey, boy," I say, putting out my hand for him to sniff.

I remember the piece of bologna I put in my pocket for a late-night snack, and I tear off a few pieces for him.

"Now he's your friend for life, dude," Yipsy says. "Ten minutes till lights out, guys." He disappears with Mick Jagger at his heels.

We fool around with anagrams for a little while longer, but soon everyone gets bored and starts playing on their phones. Simon's quiet. He quickly throws on a pair of jogging pants and a T-shirt and gets into bed. He shoves his phone under his pillow and turns off the light that's clipped onto his headboard. He doesn't say goodnight.

Lily sometimes says the thing you can't have is

always more appealing than the thing you do have. That seems kind of pointless to me, but whenever I've asked her why she feels that way, she just tells me to stop being dense.

I try to sleep, but my head is filled with soft images of the moon and the ducks rising off the lake, of Sal cooing and Mia singing. So when I hear everyone's deep, rhythmic breathing, I slip out of bed and open my computer. Glowing in the screen's light, I open my last cinematic installment of *A Life So Far*, and the images dance across the screen.

The sixth-grade class trip to the aquarium, where I filmed Bailey doing an interpretive dance about dolphin captivity while Rex accompanied her on the didgeridoo. The class picnic where I filmed a virtual tour of the woods in search of Bigfoot sightings. Lily's school dance, where her friends lined up in the backyard for pictures while I held their bags. The talent show where I manned the punch bowl.

I upload Mia's performance from my phone and edit it in. Tomorrow night, at Show Your Stuff, I'm going to show mine.

I hear guffawing coming from outside. Peering out, careful not to be seen, I spy Mike and Jake Rottweiler, the beams of their flashlights bouncing along the ground. They're creeping across the clearing to the signpost at the camp entrance. They keep their voices low, looking around as if they don't want to be seen. Mike is holding a shovel and Jake is holding a burlap sack.

Suddenly, Mike glances up in my direction as if he senses me watching him. I duck, and after a few seconds, they turn and trot up the path toward the historic homestead site.

What are they doing out so late at night, and where are they going?

My thoughts spin with curiosity, but as I crawl back into my bunk, a tidal wave of *tired* crashes over me. Before I know it, I'm fast asleep.

CHAPTER 10

The next morning, I can't stop thinking about Pops's notes, the anagrams, and the Rottweilers. But I'm also stoked about Showing My Stuff after dinner. I hope Mia likes my opus.

In the mess hall, I spot her a few tables over with her bunkmates, and my heart does a little flip. The other girls swipe at their phones and laugh. Mia chews and stares into space. Every few seconds, she checks her phone, then stares into space some more.

After piling food onto our breakfast trays, Simon, Tyler, Josh, and I grab seats, and it isn't long before the conversation becomes all about Pops's mysterious notes.

"Maybe Sal will deliver another one later," Tyler says, sprinkling salt on his eggs.

"Does he usually come at night?" Josh asks, drowning his waffles in syrup.

"So far, he's come once at night and once during the day," I remark, chomping on my toast.

"Hmm." Josh ponders this. "Night is better. Draws less attention to you, Noah."

"Yeah." Tyler nods, leans in, and speaks low. "I also think we should probably keep this to ourselves."

"Agreed," says Simon. "It's a little weird."

"And you don't want people butting in—putting it all over social media and stuff," Josh says. "You don't want to attract attention from the FBI."

"The FBI?" I exclaim. "Why would they care about Sal and me?"

"Well, duh," Josh says. "A dorky kid—no offense—is getting secret messages from a carrier pigeon about saving the world. It's the stuff of superhero comics."

I grin. "I kind of like that idea."

"Not in real life, you wouldn't. Nobody wants the FBI on their tail," Josh says solemnly. "Trust me."

"He knows what he's talking about," Tyler says as a spindle of cereal milk drips down his chin.

I kind of doubt that Josh knows much about the

FBI, but what's the point of having friends if you don't at least try to believe them?

"Hey, maybe after lights out, we can sneak out and toss some bread crumbs around," Tyler suggests. "Ya know, coax Sal out."

"I don't think Sal wants food," I say. "I think he comes when he has a message. What do you think, Simon? Simon?"

Simon doesn't answer. He just stares across the room.

The target of his gaze is Lily. She acts like she doesn't know she's being watched, but every few seconds her eyes dart up in Simon's direction.

I may not be good at reading every room, but I can read Lily pretty well. The more a guy stares at her, the more she flips her hair, reapplies her lip gloss, and pretends that she's only interested in her friends. This can only mean one thing.

"I think she likes you," I say, nudging my leaky eggs with my fork to keep them from soggy-ing up my toast.

"You think so?" Simon breaks into a big smile.

Josh barks a laugh and spritzes juice through his nose.

Tyler pretends to kiss his waffle.

"I love you!" Josh bats his eyes at his spoon, then crushes it against his chest.

"Shut up," Simon snaps.

"Dude," Josh says. "It's cool. She's cute."

"Yeah," Tyler nods. "Besides, watching you crush on a girl is better than watching you swipe through your phone all summer."

"Who are you swiping?" Lily suddenly appears next to us, holding her tray. Her friends huddle up behind her.

"He's swiping his mates in London," I answer.

"His *mates?*" Lily says the word like she's tasting it on her tongue. "Is that, like, an English word?"

Her friends grin and nudge each other with their trays.

"Don't you like American words?" she asks him flirtatiously.

Simon blushes and puts his phone in his pocket. He opens his mouth and then closes it, like he's trying to think of something interesting to say but can't. He finally comes up with "I like all words."

"Oh." Lily frowns and starts toward the other table. "Well, see you at the lake . . . Oh, hi, Noah, what's up?"

She doesn't wait for an answer.

"Well, that was smooth," Josh says to Simon.

After breakfast, we gather around the flagpole. Mick Jagger waggles up to me for a lick and I give him the few linty crackers I have in my pocket. He chomps them up, then waggles back to Yipsy, who's wearing a yellow baseball cap that says *Yipsy* across the rim in big, blue letters.

Nurse Leibowitz stands beside him looking like a giant red blot in her matching velour leggings and hoodie. Her hands rest on the black medical bag locked and loaded across her chest, and she narrows her eyes at us like she suspects we're carrying some killer germs that she's armed to snuff out.

"Why is Yipsy wearing a hat with his name on it?" says Josh.

"In case he gets lost and someone has to bring him back," Simon says. "Pardon me!" He puckers up his face and speaks in a high voice. "Does this Yipsy belong to you?"

This makes us laugh, and I'm glad that Simon seems happier.

From the corner of my eye, I spy Mia by a cluster of pine trees. She's sitting in a cross-legged yoga position, her palms resting on her knees and facing up, her eyes closed, and her face tilted toward the sky. Today the bottom fringe of her hair is lilac-colored.

Simon nudges me. "Why don't you go talk to her?"

"Who?"

"You know ruddy well who." He shoves me, and I stumble forward. "Go ahead," he urges me.

I amble over to Mia, trying to look real casual.

"Hey, Mia." My voice squeaks.

Her eyes open and flit in my direction. She sighs in a way that sounds annoyed.

"Hey," she says and glances toward her bunk-mates at the volleyball court. "Be right there!" She waves to them.

They're talking to some guys from Bunk 2 and don't even glance over.

"That's Trina, Marisa, and Jill, but she spells it with a 'y' and two 'll's like Jyll," Mia says. "I think that's brave."

"I really liked your song the other night," I say. "It was cool, all about the dying earth and stuff."

"Thanks." She smiles. "It's a new one. Song 42."

"You number your songs?" I ask. "How come?"

"I got the idea from that Beatles song, 'Number 9.' It inspired me. Have you ever heard it?"

"Sure," I say.

No.

"It's easier to categorize the songs when you number them," she continues, "and it not only reminds me of the transcendental creative flow, but it's an ironic homage to the impact and temporality of words. Know what I mean?"

"Totally." I nod vigorously.

No again.

She shoots me a suspicious sidelong glance. "You do? Really?"

"I name my opuses."

"Your what?" she says curiously.

"My opuses. My most important work. Those are the film installments of my life so far. They're called *A Life So Far.*" I point to the camera headpiece I'm wearing. "See?"

"Right," she says. "I remember from the bus."

"You do?" I brighten.

"Yeah. That's, um, clever, I guess."

"You think so?" I say. "I'm also into *cinéma vérité.* That's—"

"Yeah, I know what that is," she interrupts, rolling up her little rubber yoga mat and squashing it under her arm.

"Maybe I can show you some of my opuses sometime," I say.

Her eyes settle on me for a moment in a way that seems like she might say yes, but then they slide over to her bunkmates, and she frowns. Mark and Dave from Bunk 3 are showing Trina, Marisa, and Jyll-with-a-y something on their phones.

"No way!" "You're gross!" and "Shut up!" Marisa and Jyll shriek, giggle, and playfully slap the guys' arms.

"My friends are waiting for me," Mia says.

"Really?" I remark. "Because it looks like they don't even know you're—"

"I said, they're waiting," Mia repeats slowly, shooting me a fiery look.

She marches off to join them, sidles up to Mark, and points to his phone.

"That's ridiculous!" she shrieks really loudly and punches him awkwardly in the arm.

Her bunkmates go quiet and clear their throats.

"Ouch." Mark rubs his arm.

Simon appears beside me. "How'd it go, mate?"

"Great!" I exclaim. "Mia numbers her songs kind of like I name my opuses. And she might just let me show her mine."

"Say what now?" His eyebrows arch up.

"My opus."

"Oh. Brilliant." Simon nods and throws his arm around my shoulder. "Now, let's go see what else is happening at the ever-interesting Camp C."

CHAPTER 11

Day One at Camp C is full of activities. First on the agenda: Morning Flagpole Seminar with Rabbi and Mrs. Blum. A few mornings a week, after breakfast, Rabbi Blum does a ten-minute presentation where he talks about something Jewish and gives us a thought for the day.

Unfortunately, it's already super hot, and we're all squirming around, wanting to get on with our activities. Mrs. Blum sweeps her eyes across the clusters of kids, and I guess she's good at reading rooms. She jokes about how the rabbi gets so excited sharing his ideas that sometimes he loses track of time. She promises to set the alarm on his phone for exactly ten minutes. This creates a wave of chuckles, and our moods lift.

This morning, the rabbi's talk is called "Moses and Me."

"Now, you kids might be thinking, *Hey!*" the Rabbi exclaims dramatically. "*Moses was a great hero. He was something really special. Not like you or me.* But guess what?!"

There's a long silence as he slides his gaze around, trying make eye contact.

"Well, I'll tell you what," he proceeds earnestly. "Moses was once just an ordinary kid too. *But, Rabbi,* you might be asking, *how could that be? Then how on earth did he get to be Moshe Rabbeinu, the teacher and hero of the Jewish people?* How many of you were thinking that? Show of hands?" The rabbi holds up his metallic coffee cup to prompt us.

"Raise your hand," Josh hisses, prompts us with his elbow, and shoots his hand up.

"But I wasn't thinking that," I whisper.

"I'll raise my hand," Simon says. "What? It's interesting."

I glance over at Mia. She's leaning back on her arms, with her legs stretched out in front of her and her face up to the sun. I wonder if she's thinking about Moses or composing a new song in her head. I wonder if maybe she's thinking about me.

"Well, I'll tell you how that could be," the rabbi says with a flourish. "It's because every one of us can be a teacher and can do good by doing . . . what?!"

"Mitzvot!" Simon shouts.

"That's right!" the rabbi shouts back.

We all turn to stare at Simon.

"I read the website," he says, smiling smugly.

"By helping other people, even by doing something small that adds value to someone's life." The rabbi talks some more, and I kind of tune out until I hear him say, "You do *tikkun olam*, helping to fix what's wrong in the world."

At that moment, a loud version of "Sunrise, Sunset" blares from his phone.

"Lake time!" Josh says.

The rest of the campers quickly collect their stuff and bolt toward the shore. I glance back over at Mia, who's trotting to catch up with her bunkmates.

I think about what the rabbi said about *tikkun olam*. Mia sort of does that with her passion for the environment and her songs about the dangers of burping plastic.

My mind snaps to Pops and his messages about saving the world. Could it be true? Could I really help save the world? Would that make me a hero of the Jewish people? I never actually thought about being a hero, but it might be nice. It would have to be a hobby, though, because I don't want to give up my filmmaking career.

Nathan slides up beside me, walking down the path to the lake in lockstep with me.

"Hey, Noah," he says.

He's wearing a loose, faded T-shirt and those big cargo shorts, with not one but three paperbacks sticking out of different pockets.

"So I was wondering if you've given any thought to your Bar Mitzvah project," he says.

I shrug. "Not really."

"Okay." He nods.

Everyone's chattering and laughing, jumping into different activities, climbing into rowboats and paddle boats, slapping balls over the water polo net, swinging out over the water in tree tires, whooping with glee as they belly-flop into the lake. Simon catches my eye and waves me over to the shore, where he's climbing into a canoe.

I glance toward Nathan, but he's just staring with a longing expression at a group of counselors. He seems particularly interested in Janine, who looks kind of cute in her red bathing suit and white shorts. The big pair of gold-framed sunglasses resting on her head reminds me of a crown.

I feel bad leaving him. "We're going canoeing," I say. "You wanna come?"

"Me?" His big brown eyes slide over to mine. "I don't like the sun. I burn easily."

"Then how do you do any activities if you don't go in the sun?"

"I mostly do inside activities," he answers. "Aside from helping with pre-Bar and Bat Mitzvah consultations, I teach Not Your Parents' Kabbalah."

"Oh." I nod.

"It's the study of mystical Judaism," he says. "In case you don't know, that's an ancient spiritual discipline that focuses on improving the world through mystical interpretations of sacred works."

"Oh." I nod again.

Huh? I think.

"Noah!" Josh shouts. He secures his life vest and waves his arms around in big circles.

"See?" Nathan says, showing me the cover of one of his books. It shows a shadowy drawing of an old white-haired guy.

"This is a book about Rabbi Isaac Luria," Nathan says happily. "He was a philosopher who lived in the sixteenth century. It's very, very interesting."

It doesn't look even a little interesting.

"Is it?" I say, hoping that he knows I'm being kind of rhetorical and won't answer.

"Jewish philosophy sometimes gets a bad rap," Nathan says, "People think it's boring and antiquated. But that's not true."

"No?" I say, glancing toward the lake, feeling the heat of the sun pounding down on my head, imagining how awesome it will feel when the cold lake water hits my skin.

"It's like what my dad was talking about—*tikkun olam*," he continues. "Repairing the world. See, this Rabbi Isaac Luria from the sixteenth century, he kind of came up with the whole idea. They called him Ari the Lion. And there was all this stuff about divine light and shards of good and evil. It's fascinating," Nathan says excitedly. "But the thing is, it's not just esoteric, out-there, like, woo-woo philosophy." He wiggles his fingers in the air. "The basic concepts can be distilled into the simple idea of mitzvot. Doing good in everyday, real life."

"Oh, real life," I nod. "I hear that. I'm a filmmaker, and I make *cinéma vérité*. That means 'real life.'" I lean down and swish my hair to the side to show him my camera.

"Hmm. Ingenious."

"NOAH! We're pushing off!" Simon shouts, stepping into the boat behind the other kids. "LAST CALL!"

"Listen, I gotta go," I say, gesturing to the lake. "It's time for my activity."

Nathan cups his hand over his eyes and squints toward the water.

"That's okay," he says, looking a little deflated. "Hey, maybe for your Bar Mitzvah project, you could make a documentary covering a social issue or something," he calls after me.

And while I'm sprinting toward the shore, it hits me. Maybe for my Bar Mitzvah project, I could save the world.

CHAPTER 12

Canoeing for Dummies starts out awesome until Lainie from Bunk 7 rows in circles so fast that it makes Mark from Bunk 11 throw up chunks of breakfast that land on his friend, who also throws up. By this time, everyone is screaming and jumping into the lake with their clothes on.

During Graphic Design for Kids, Mark from Bunk 11 googles "gross stuff," which brings up sites about toe fungus, poop larvae, and even grosser stuff—until Brett, the counselor from Bunk 9, threatens to call our parents.

Next we have soccer, where I foul out a bunch of times and trip myself once. But before I even hit the ground, Nurse Leibowitz is leaning over me, blocking out the entire sun, dabbing my knee with some smelly ointment that stings.

After that comes water polo, where Josh gets hit in the eye with the ball, and in like two seconds, Nurse Leibowitz is back, half-marching and half-butt-sliding down the embankment.

"Out of my way. Out of my way," she commands even though no one is in her way. "Where's the patient?"

"I guess that would be me, but I'm really fi—" Josh tries to say while she takes his temperature, checks his blood pressure, and listens to his heart.

"It's actually just my eye." Josh tries to squirm away. "And it's not that big a dea—"

"Quiet," Nurse Leibowitz snaps, leaning in close, shining a light into his pupils.

"It doesn't even hur—" he starts.

"Infirmary!" She shuts him down.

"But—"

"Infirmary. Now!"

"She's tough," Simon whispers to me.

"Can I at least change out of my swim—" Josh whimpers as she leads him by the arm up the embankment.

"Later," Nurse Leibowitz barks.

"Help me," Josh mouths, shooting us a pleading look over his shoulder.

Finally, it's Environment and You, and that's the best. Mia's there, sitting in the back, with Trina, Marisa, and Jyll yakking about new hair products and healthy snacks. Mia's hair looks pretty—loose and bouncy. Every few seconds she's like, "What?"

And "Who?"

And "Whaddaya mean?"

And "Yeah, me too, totally!"

When the counselor starts talking about plant studies and how plants have feelings, Mia gets all amped until Jyll is like, "I hope you're not suggesting I don't eat salads, because that is so not happening."

Mia looks crestfallen, so I shoot her a supportive look and go, "I like plants."

"You would," Trina sneers at me, and Jyll and Marisa laugh.

Mia doesn't say anything for the rest of the class, even though she clears her throat a bunch of times like she's going to say something and shifts restlessly in her seat.

Finally, it's time for the evening campfire roast, storytime, and sing-along.

It's a dark, misty kind of night, and the campfire spits and smokes, illuminating the woodsy sky with orange light. Mick Jagger runs over to me, and I feed him a piece of a tofurky hot dog. He barks appreciatively until Yipsy whistles for him.

"New friend?" Simon asks. "Any messages tied to him?"

I wonder when I'm gonna get another message from Sal and if the world still needs saving. I think about *tikkun olam*, repairing the world, and Ari the Lion. It's funny that saving the world was a thing even in the sixteenth century. I would have thought most people were more worried about having a place to sleep and where their next piece of matzah was coming from and whether the Cossacks were coming to kick them out of their homes.

It hits me that maybe some people are just wired to worry about bigger things than themselves. I think about Mia and how socially conscious she is. I'm not sure if I'm wired to save the world, but think it might be cool to care about something bigger than myself.

By the campfire, Josh and Tyler roast marshmallows and pull strings of goo from their sticks with their teeth. Simon veers off in the direction of Lily and her friends while texts ping on his phone. I'm looking for Mia when Mike Rottweiler knocks right into me.

"Omph!" I stumble forward, causing him to splash his drink onto both of us.

"Hey, watch it!" he erupts.

"Sorry."

"You're in my way," he says.

Jake sidles up to Mike. I'm frantically trying to get someone's attention with my eyes.

"Was that you watching us from your cabin window the other night?" Mike asks.

"Yeah, you spying on us?" Jake adds.

"You filming us?" Mike bites out, holding his red plastic cup halfway to his open mouth, piercing me with his gaze.

"Um . . . no?" I say.

"What? What do you mean, Turtle?" Mike snarls, moving close up into my grill. "Were you spying on us or not?"

"Are you asking, or is that rhetorical?" I say.

"You being smart?" Mike shoves me.

Jake shoves me from the back. "Whatsa matter?" he growls, his eyes gleaming with meanness. "Where are your friends now?"

I'm wondering the same thing as I'm being violently bounced back and forth between them. I feel like one of Mick Jagger's toys when he grabs it by the neck, shakes it hard, tosses it across the room, pounces on it, and starts again.

No one seems to notice what's going on, and everyone around me is just a blur of colors and faces.

"Yeah, no one likes a smart butt." Jake pushes.

"Yeah, no one." Mike pushes. "Or a freakin' spy."

"I—leave me alone—" I stammer, fighting pin-pricks of tears.

"Ooh, he's gonna cry," Mike sneers.

"You gonna cry?" Jake taunts, then shoves me hard back into Mike.

"I—" My teeth are rattling now. "I'd like not to."

"Spy on us again and you'll really have some-thing to cry about." Mike shoves me harder.

"And if I see your camera anywhere near us, you'll be crying for days." Jake slaps my head.

Out of nowhere, Simon, Josh, and Tyler appear.

"Leave him alone," says Simon.

"Yeah," Josh says, although he's much less con-vincing than Simon.

"I've got this," I say, my voice all warbly, as Jake and Mike continue to bat me around.

"I said let him go." Simon steps in closer.

The Rottweilers pause. They're big, strong, and hairy, but Simon is super athletic.

Their eyes slide from Simon to Tyler to Josh, and there's a hot second when I don't know what they're gonna do.

"Simon is very good at soccer," I say, taking a quick swipe at my wet cheek with my shoulder.

Jake snorts a laugh. "Does anyone ever know what this kid is talking about?"

Simon chest-butts up against Mike and levels a feral gaze at him.

"Whoa, take it easy, Brit boy." Mike backs up and lifts his palms.

"Hey, what's going on here?" Lily is suddenly at my side, and a little crowd is gathering around us now.

"Oooh, now you got a girl defending you?" Mike sneers. "Hey, cute thing."

"Shut up, butt wipe," Lily snaps.

"Oh, I'm scared." Jake pretends to shrink away.

"Yeah, don't hit me with your purse!" Mike laughs.

"How about I hit you with my fist?" Lily says challengingly. "Self-defense class teaches empowerment *and* is a great workout."

Now Yipsy is pushing his way toward us, with Janine, Cooper, Sarah, and Nathan following close behind. Mick Jagger barks wildly at their heels.

"What's going on?" Yipsy demands.

In the sea of faces, I spot Mia and her bunkmates.

"Ugh, not that kid again," Jyll sneers in my direction.

"Let's go." Trina rolls her eyes. She and the other two spin on their heels. "Mia, you coming?"

Mia chews her lip uncertainly, then follows them.

"Everything's fine, Yipsy," Simon finally says.

Yipsy looks like he's processing this, maybe trying to figure out if we're telling the truth.

"We were just leaving, right, Jake?" Mike smiles sweetly at Yipsy, then brushes hard against my shoulder as he makes his way to the fire pit.

"Okay, cool." Yipsy bops his head up and down, looking kind of relieved. "Come on, the marshmallows are getting cold."

"How can marshmallows get cold?" I ask.

The crowd starts to disperse, except for Nathan.

"You okay, Noah?" he asks, looking shaken up.

Before I can answer, Lily turns on me angrily. "Oh my God, Noah. What were you doing?!"

"Nothing," I say in a small, guilty voice.

"They won't bother him again." Simon straightens and rolls his shoulders back. "He'll be fine."

"Uh-huh." Lily looks skeptical. "Of course he's fine. He's always fine. I'm the one who's not fine. Noah, we need to talk."

Mick Jagger barks, wags, and dances around Lily's feet.

"Ugh," she says, trying to disengage from him. "Could you please tell your new friend to heel or something?"

"Find Yipsy!" I command, pointing toward the flagpole.

"Okay," Nathan says, turns, and zips away.

"I was talking to Mick Jagger!" I call out after him.

Lily grabs my arm and spins me around. "How am I supposed to have any fun if you keep getting into trouble?"

"I'm not in trouble, Lily."

She stares at me for a few moments while the light of the fire, like a strobe, accents a bunch of emotions streaking across her face. I can't read her room at all.

"Why do I bother?" she says softly, more to herself than to anyone else.

"I don't know," I say.

Her expression settles into the stony, indifferent mask I know pretty well. She turns to Simon with the kind of smile that doesn't reach her eyes.

"It was really nice of you to watch out for him," she says.

"We were here, too." Josh raises his hand. Tyler nods.

"Later," Lily says as she flips her hair and pivots toward her friends. But not before glancing at Simon one more time.

"What was going on with you and those Rotties?" Simon frowns at me.

"They were creeping around the woods the other night, and they think I was spying on them," I say.

"Were you?" Josh asks.

"Sort of."

"What were they doing?" Tyler says.

"Don't know." I shrug. "But it might be something bad. And maybe," I add, thinking aloud, "we should try and find out."

CHAPTER 13

The next night, the mess hall sounds like a hundred buzzing bees. I find Yipsy at the counselors' table eating a big bowl of chicken noodle soup, trying to stab a bobbing matzah ball with his spoon.

"Hey, Noah," he says, wiping broth from his beard, missing a few strands of noodles that hang there like worms. "What can I do for you?"

"I want to show my opus."

"Hmmm." He frowns. "I'm not following, little bro."

"Show my stuff," I say.

"Oh!" He brightens and goes to slap me five, which I do, even though his fingers are slimy, because it's awkward not to slap someone five when they offer. I explain what he needs to do and give him the thumb drive containing my opus.

Back at the table, I'm too excited to eat. Mia's in the corner with her bunkmates, but I can't seem to catch her attention.

"What's up with you?" Simon narrows his eyes at me suspiciously. "You look like you have a secret."

"You'll see," I say, grinning.

Lily is sitting with her friends a few seats down, but I must have activated her bro-dar because her head snaps up in my direction.

"What kind of secret, Noah? What's going on?" Lily puts down her fork and frowns at me.

"Nothing," I lie.

"Noah," she says in a warning tone that reminds me of Mom.

"He'll be okay." Simon talks to Lily like he's already her boyfriend, which worries me. She might like him, but she's not that loyal. When I was little, I used to think I was important to her too.

When we're all done eating, Yipsy is like, "Okay, everyone, it's time for . . ." He cups his hand behind his ear.

Nothing.

"Come on, I can't hear you. It's time for . . ."

"Not this again." Josh slaps his hand to his head.

Big belches emanate from the Rottweilers' table, followed by snorting laughter and guffaws.

"Me!" I exclaim.

"All right!" Yipsy smiles wide. "Noah is gonna show us his stuff. Cool!"

"Noah." Lily leans toward me. "Whatever you're thinking, it's probably not a good idea."

"How do you know?" I ask. "And what do you care?"

For a second she looks all surprised and hurt. "I care," she says softly.

"Yeah, right," I say in my best sarcastic voice. Because all of a sudden, I'm feeling pretty freakin' good.

"Noah, come on down!" Yipsy gestures at me, wheeling a TV and an attached laptop into place.

Mia cocks her head in my direction. Wait until she sees this!

Someone lowers the lights, and my opus begins.

All the images from *A Life So Far* flash across the screen: the aquarium, the Bigfoot hunt, the sixth-grade dance—all the most important bits from the last year. I'm nervous and excited, and it feels like time is slow and fast at the same time. My heartbeat pounds in my ears.

Mia flashes onto the screen, sitting on her stool, staring coolly into the crowd, her voice once again filling the room.

It's quiet for a few moments until I hear snickering and whispering. My stomach flips a little. From the corner of my eye, I spot Mia, who's staring at the screen—not laughing, not smiling, not doing anything.

"Pretty lame," someone says in a low voice.

Suddenly Val from Bunk 7 rushes in, shouting, "Hey, there's a rugelach-eating contest down by the volleyball court! Woot!"

There's a bunch of "Woot! Woot! Woot!"

Chairs scrape across the wood floor and everyone stampedes out. But my opus isn't over and, on the screen, Mia's voice warbles on. The only people in the room are me, Yipsy, Mia, and Mick Jagger, who's happily thrashing his fuzzy toy cat. Mia stares blankly at the screen, and I can't read her room at all.

Yipsy leans over and presses pause on the computer. Mick drops his toy at my feet and pants up at me.

"Um, that was cool, dude," Yipsy says, placing his arm around my shoulder.

Mia stands abruptly and bolts out the door.

I'm not sure exactly what happened, but the moment I leave the mess hall, Lily grabs my arm and drags me to an isolated spot by the trees. It's almost 8:00, and the sky looks like runny paint of deep blues.

"Noah, jeez!" she explodes. "I mean, like, what were you thinking showing your My Life Right Now thingie? And why did you edit in that weird growly girl? Are you trying to ruin my summer?"

"No."

"Well, I think you are," she hisses.

"Maybe I should change it up," I say to Lily. "Or edit it differently. Put Mia first, then Bailey's interpretive dance at the aquarium, then the Bigfoot search next, then—"

"Noah!" Lily barks.

"What?"

But she just stares at me.

"For the rest of the summer? Just, like, don't talk to me, okay?" She stomps off.

What was that about? I'm standing alone, listening to woodsy chirping, when I catch sight of Mia over by the trees.

"Hey!" I approach her. "Whaddaya think? The reaction was a little . . . unusual, but I think you looked awesome on the screen."

Mia turns away, swiping at her eyes, smudging her black mascara.

"Are you crying?" I ask.

"No," she sniffs.

"About my opus?"

She doesn't say anything.

"That's so awesome!" I say.

"I'm not crying because I liked your film. I'm crying because I hated it."

"Oh. I just . . . I just didn't film it right," I stammer.

"I don't sound like that. Or look like that," she squeaks, waving her hand dismissively in the air.

"But you do," I say.

"I don't," she repeats, her voice all shaky.

"Um . . . yeah, you do," I say. "But it's cool."

"You're just . . . weird," Mia snaps.

"So are you," I say.

"I am not."

"Yeah, you are," I insist. "But that's why I like you. You're different than other kids."

"I'm not!" she explodes, leaning close into my face, her eyes dark and angry. "And I don't like when you say that. Don't say that. I'm just like my friends."

Our eyes swing over to Trina, Marisa, and Jyll.

They're throwing rugelach at each other and laughing their heads off.

"See?" Mia sniffs defensively.

"No." I frown.

"I'm only nice to you because you're weird and have no friends," she snaps, wiping at her watery nose.

"I have mates," I say.

"And you shouldn't make movies about people," she continues, "and not tell them."

"It's *cinéma vérité*. The truth."

"I don't care," Mia responds. "I have to go. My friends are waiting."

She storms away and I feel—I don't know. I can't even read my own room. I need time to think. So I walk briskly past the pine trees, away from the chatter and laughter of the campfire, to a place that's quiet.

At that moment, I hear the sounds of wings flapping toward me. It's Sal! He swoops in, lands on my shoulder, and hops onto my hand. A small, raggedy piece of paper flaps on his leg.

I detach the note. It says: *Look behind you.*

CHAPTER 14

"Psst!"

"Who's there?!" I spin around, alarmed.

"Pssssttt!"

I part the bushes and climb over tree stumps, trying to follow the voice, heading deeper into the woods.

"Pssttt!" The voice is insistent now.

"Who is it?" I say.

"Ned!" the voice whispers hoarsely.

What the . . . ! Could it be? "Pops?"

I step into a clearing and, sure enough, there's Pops sitting on a rock. He's wearing what looks like some kind of old-guy Boy Scout uniform: beige shorts, a beige button-down shirt, black socks, and white sneakers. He holds a kerosene lantern and squints into the darkness.

"Pops? What are you doing here?"

"Didn't you get my pigeon?" Pops responds, standing too fast and promptly falling back down onto the rock. "Help me up."

I rush to grab his arm and pull him to his feet.

"Well?" he demands.

"Well what?" I say. "You mean all those messages tied to Sal's foot about saving the world?"

"Who's Sal?"

"That's what I named your pigeon. After your friend from the army."

"Well, I guess it's better than calling him Pigeon," Pops remarks.

We stand in silence for a few moments.

"Enough of your chatter." He throws his hands up in exasperation. Next, he makes a creaky three-sixty circle, holding his lamp up high and peering out into the woods.

"We have to be careful so nobody hears us," he says secretively.

"Pops, what's going on?"

A tree branch cracks.

"Get down," Pops hisses, yanking me into a crouch position next to him.

"Pops, your lantern is pretty bright," I whisper.

"You're right." He drags me toward one of the docked canoes, crouches down behind it, and yanks me down with him. "Pretend you're an owl. *Hoot, hoot*," he sings deep and low.

"But—"

"Do it!"

"*Hoot, hoot, hoot*," we both hoot.

"Pops, this is dumb," I interrupt. "We don't sound like owls. We sound like weird people pretending to be owls."

"Shh," he murmurs. "It's a stealth technique I learned in the Secret Service."

A familiar voice rings out: "Noah!"

"Over here." I straighten up.

"Get down, get down!" Pops yanks at the waist of my shorts, pulling them below my hips.

"Hey!" I grab for my waistband.

"Get down," Pops insists. "*Hoot, hoot!*"

"Oh, no," the voice with a clipped British accent says. "It can't be."

"Over here!" I try to disentangle myself from Pops's steely grip. Man, what do they feed him at Shady Pines? "Stop it, Pops." I struggle. "It's just Simon. You met him at your birthday party. He's the kid from London."

"Is he in on it too?! Drat! *Hoot, hoot, hoot.*"

"Simon!" I yell.

The beam from Simon's flashlight bounces toward us.

"Noah? Is that you?"

"Yeah . . . Let go, Pops," I grunt, trying to wriggle away. "It's okay. We can get up."

"Mr. Pops?" Simon gapes. "What are you doing here?"

"I'm here," he says, "to save the world. What else?"

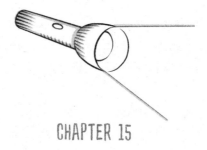

CHAPTER 15

"I found him in the woods," I tell Simon.

Pops grabs our arms and pulls us behind the trees. "I thought you were in Florida, Pops," I say.

"I was," Pops replies dismissively. "I needed to lay low for a while, get away and think."

"About what?" Simon asks.

"What am I talking about here?!" Pop exclaims impatiently.

"We don't really kn—" I start.

"Besides," he goes on, "your Aunt Phyllis was driving me nuts. Wanted me to hang around with old fogeys and play shuffleboard and bingo." He barks a sarcastic laugh. "As if that's all I have to do with my time."

"What else *do* you have to do with your time?" I ask.

"Don't be sassy," Pops snaps. "Now, the answer," he continues, "is in these very woods."

"Pops, I've been thinking a lot about saving the world. And I want you to know that I'm in. I mean, I'm completely on board with it," I declare, looking into Pops's face with what I hope is great conviction. "I want to save people, even people I don't know. Ya know, do good. *Tikkun olam*. Like Moses and Ari the Lion."

"Ah, yes," Simon concurs. "That would be elevating."

"Are we too late?" I ask anxiously.

But before he can answer, we hear another voice.

"Hey! You guys back here?" Tyler shouts.

"Watcha doin'?" Josh yells. "Yipsy's starting team Scattergories. He'll freak if he notices you're gone."

"We're—" I start, but Pops clamps his hand over my face.

I have to pry his Vapo-Rub-smelling fingers from my mouth. "It's okay, Pops! They're my friends."

"Everyone is your friend," Pops says. "That's the problem. You're too trusting. How can you save the world if you *like* everyone?"

Lily's annoyed-sounding voice rings out. "I told you he's probably back at the bunk."

"Nope, looked there," Josh says.

"Noah!" she yells. "Don't you know the woods are dangerous? Get out of there before I kill you!"

"It's Lily, Pops," I say. "See?"

I point to the three of them turning the wrong way on the path, padding out of sight.

"Now, listen, Ned. You too, Hippie. This is important." Pops leans in close to us, his breath smelling like kosher pickles. "Meet me here tomorrow at five in the morning"

"*Is* there a five in the morning?" Simon jokes.

"That's super early, Pops. And we have activities," I say. "Can't you tell us *now* about how to save the world?"

Pops shakes his head vigorously. "Not here. Not now," he says. "Very soon, though. Let's make it ten in the morning. Sharp."

"Sure, better," we mumble on top of each other.

"Just so you know," Pops says, "you'll need to bring shovels, picks, burlap sacks, and sandwiches."

"We don't have shovels, picks, or burlap sacks," I respond.

He nods. "Fine, I'll bring 'em."

"Are you ever gonna tell us what this is all about?" I sigh.

"Okay, fine," Pops grumbles irritably. "I'll tell you a few things. There's a secret from World War II that's buried here, on the site of the Levy Homestead. It will reveal . . ."

Pops looks solemn and points up.

"The sky?" Simon says quizzically.

"Nope."

"The moon?" I guess.

"Nope."

"The stars?" I try again.

"Nope."

"Oh, wait, I'm rather good at charades," Simon says. "What does it sound like?"

"Asteroid." Pops's voice is grave.

"Asteroid, asteroid," Simon ponders. "C'asteroid, D'asteroid, F'asteroid . . . hmm . . . I don't know."

"Asteroid! Asteroid is the word!" Pops exclaims. "Don't they teach you hippies anything at the commune? A giant asteroid is about to destroy Earth!"

"What?!" I explode.

"In a few weeks' time." Pops leans in close. "That baby will crash right into us. And *splat*! We'll all be flatter than Aunt Phyllis's matzah brei. But we can do something about it."

"We can stop an asteroid?" Simon asks.

I stare hard into Pops's face. Has he gone completely bonkers? But he looks the same as he always has, which may or may not be a bad thing. Is it possible that any of this is true?

"Mr. Pops," Simon says gently as if he's talking to a little kid. "This outer space talk. Does it have anything to do with aliens? Do you ever watch television shows about aliens? Say, maybe, when you're tired late at night or after you've taken your medication?"

"Aliens?!" Pops snaps. "What are you talking about? Have you flipped your cap? And the only medication I take is for my hemorrhoids."

Without warning, a flashlight beam bounces into my face, blinding me. Is it the FBI? An alien hunter?! An alien?! I'm freaking out!

"For God's sake, Noah!" Lily squints into the dark void but doesn't see us. "What are you doing now? You really are bent on ruining my summer, frizzing out my hair, and giving me a heart attack, aren't you? And who are you whispering to?"

Her voice fades as she heads in another wrong direction.

"Hmmph," Pop grumbles. "I'm going to bed."

Simon and I exchange confused looks.

"Now?" I say.

"Why not?" Pops says. "It's nighttime, isn't it?"

"Um, will you be residing in the woods, Mr. Pops?" Simon asks.

"Of course not. I'm staying at the motel up the road. But don't go telling all your 'friends,'" Pops says, making air quotation marks around the word *friends*. "Because this is dangerous, and I don't want anyone knowing where I am."

"Pops, wait!" I call out after him.

"Ach." He waves at us dismissively. "The road is just up ahead. Somewhere."

"Do you at least have a compass?" Simon probes.

"A compass? What is this, 1971?" Pop grumbles. "I have Google Maps. This place is crawling with Wi-Fi. Got an Uber waiting for me too."

And with that, he disappears into the woods.

CHAPTER 16

Right before we reach our bunk, Simon slips off to call his mates. I'm about to head up to the screen door when a voice behind me stops me in my tracks.

"Hey!"

"Whaa?" I jump and spin around.

"Sorry," Nathan says, standing there looking kind of sheepish. "Did I scare you?"

"No," I say.

Yes, I think, and I suddenly realize how late it is.

"Are we, like, in trouble?" I ask.

"Trouble?" Nathan echoes, like he hadn't even thought of it. "Why?"

"'Cause it's so late? Isn't there, like, a curfew?"

From the corner of my eye, I notice Josh and Tyler inside the cabin, bunched around the window, frantically shaking their heads and mouthing the word "no."

"I mean—um." I hesitate. "I'll be back earlier next time."

More frantic head-shaking from my mates. And Nathan is frowning at me like he thinks I'm weird.

"I mean . . ." My eyes keep darting to the window for advice. "I was in the woods . . . I thought I saw an animal . . ."

The guys are going nuts now, mouthing "shut up," making slash signs across their throats, and wildly shaking their heads.

"Like, a wild animal?" Nathan says, looking worried.

I'm a terrible liar! This is all making me so nervous! My armpits are getting sticky, and I have to loudly gulp down a big wad of saliva that's lodged in my throat.

"I mean, I thought I saw a wild animal, but it was really just Mick Jagger," I offer weakly. "Then I decided to film him. Ya know, running."

I tilt my head down so Nathan can see my camera.

"It looks like it's off," Nathan says suspiciously.

The guys at the window are slapping their heads and looking like they're in agony.

Nathan's eyes snap up to the window, but Josh and Tyler duck just in time.

"I . . ." I start, my eyes welling up now. "I don't know what I'm saying. I'm lying. I don't know why."

"It's okay, Noah," Nathan says gently. He reaches out and gives my shoulder a few pats. "After what happened with those bullies, it's no wonder you're upset." His expression is serious. "There's a Jewish proverb that says, *Courage is a kingdom without a crown.*"

"Cool," I say, because I have no idea what he means and don't know what else to say.

"It's okay," he repeats. "You don't have to tell me what you were doing out so late."

"Whew." I let out the long breath I didn't know I was holding. "That's a relief."

We stand in silence for a few moments, and I notice that the air is rich with cricket-y night sounds. Somewhere in the distance, a lone dog howls. The hazy full moon throws soft, fuzzy light, and the sweet smell of pine is everywhere.

"The camp grounds are really safe," Nathan finally says. "Someone's always nearby, and I'm betting you all keep your phones with you. The place has great Wi-Fi."

"I've heard that," I say, thinking of Pops.

"Just don't go out there alone," he continues, "especially when Mike and Jake are wandering around."

"It's okay," I say reassuringly. "I have mates."

"I see that." Nathan smirks, darting his eyes toward the window, where Tyler and Josh again duck quickly out of sight.

"Sometimes," he sighs, his gaze traveling out toward the trees that softly sway in the warm breeze, "I like to take night walks too. Just to think."

Maybe I should tell Nathan about saving the world. I wonder what he'd think about that. But before I can say anything, he's like, "Well, 'night." He pivots and walks up to the creaky screen door of his bunk.

"I'm thinking about saving the world," I blurt out.

"What?" Nathan spins back around.

"Actually, someone I know is trying to save the world," I clarify. "But I think I'd like to help. That's like *tikkun olam*, right? And maybe that could be my Bar Mitzvah project. What a great opportunity to kill two birds with one stone, right?"

Nathan doesn't say anything for a few long moments. Finally, he looks ponderous and is like, "Hmm. That's a good thought, but it's a little general. It might be overwhelming to try to save the *whole* world at one time."

"That's a valid point," I reply. "But my friend says he has some kind of plan."

"Which is?"

"It's top secret," I say, "so I really can't tell you any more."

Nathan kicks a pebble around with his shoe, and it looks like a little smile is tugging at his lips. "Maybe you could start a little smaller, maybe doing charity for some good cause or helping with a food drive. You could make a documentary about the cause and raise money."

Josh and Tyler appear at the window again, this time making goofy faces, squishing their noses against the glass, and stuff like that. The air is getting chilly, and I think it's time to go inside.

"Um . . . no," I reply thoughtfully. "I think I'd better just jump in and save the whole world first. Then I can maybe do some kind of other mitzvot. There's a no-kill animal shelter in town. They need dog walkers."

"Well . . ." Nathan looks contemplative. "You seem pretty committed to the idea, but I think we should talk more about it. 'Kay?" And with that, Nathan walks up to the creaky screen door and disappears inside.

Later that night, lying in my bed, I'm like, *Man, do I have a lot to think about!*

First, there's the mystery with Pops. Is Earth really in danger of being smashed by a giant asteroid, and do we really only have a few weeks to live? Can we stop it? And how exactly can I get this all on film?

And then there's Mia. Why was she so upset? Is it possible that she doesn't know what she sounds like when she sings? And why would her voice make her angry? Because it's different? Is it that she likes to be different but not *too* different? Or is it that she's different in a way she didn't expect to be? I'm starting to think that no one really knows how they sound or look. And no one really knows how other people see them.

Quietly I sit up, careful not to wake Tyler and Josh. I grab the little desk mirror and stare into the small black irises of my own eyes. Maybe nobody really sees the me I want them to see either. Being a *cinéma vérité* filmmaker may help me reveal the truth in other people, but I'm still not sure what the truth is in me.

Simon slips through the screen door. "Hey, whatcha doing?" he says slowly, seeing me nose-to-nose with my own reflection.

"Trying to see the truth in my soul."

"Right." He sighs, tossing his phone onto his pillow and plopping down onto his bed. "So what's this all this rubbish with your pops?"

"What makes you think it's rubbish?" I say.

"Are you joking?" he says, his eyes widening. "You don't really believe him, do you?"

"I'm not sure, but wouldn't it be cool if he was telling the truth? I mean, even though I know it sounds impossible—"

"Ya think?"

"But what if it's real?" I persist.

"Seriously?" Simon says too loudly. Tyler shifts in his top bunk, bumping the top of my head with his butt.

"Shh," I whisper, moving next to Simon. I'm careful not to jostle Josh, who's sprawled across his bed, tangled in the covers. "It could be true."

"Noah," Simon says in a low voice, "don't you think that if Earth were in danger of being hit by some monster asteroid, the government would know about it?"

"Maybe they do," I say.

Simon's phone buzzes loudly. "Oh crap, hang on," he says. "Hello?" he says into his phone.

Josh turns over in his bed and slowly sits up, his face slack in a state of half-sleep. "'Sup?" he says hoarsely.

"Killer asteroids," Simon answers him. Into his phone, he's like, "Have to call you back. What? Football match? Dunno. Yeah, you'll figure it out without me," and he hangs up.

"Huh?" Josh says, rubbing his face and swinging his legs over the side of his bed.

"My pops thinks a giant asteroid is hurtling through space and is about to crash into Earth."

"Um . . . what?" Josh yawns and turns to Simon. "Translate, please."

Simon fills him in on everything that's happened.

"And the key to preventing it is buried somewhere on the historic site," I blurt excitedly.

"For real?" Josh asks.

"It's all nonsense, of course," Simon says.

Tyler moans and rolls over. "Shuddup, you guys. I'm trying to sleep."

Josh throws a pillow at Tyler.

"Jeez!" Tyler moans, sits up, wipes the drool from his mouth, and squints out the window. "It's the middle of the night."

"Could be true." Josh shrugs. "Maybe."

"So you believe it? That's awesome!" I exclaim.

"Whoa, don't get too excited." Josh holds up his palms. "I didn't say I believed it."

"Well, I still unequivocally don't believe it," Simon says.

"Oh, cheerio," Josh says dryly, mimicking the British accent. "Unequivocally? Speak English, dude."

"I'm saying it's all crap," Simon retorts.

Tyler puts on his glasses, slides down from his bunk, and perches on the edge of my cot. "I'm sorry, could you all explain this again?" he says.

"Dude, whew. Gum first. Open your mouth a second," Josh says, waving his hand in front of his face.

He mashes a piece of gum into his own mouth, then chucks one over to Tyler.

Simon shakes his head. "Even if it were true, that still doesn't mean it has anything to do with buried secrets or your pops."

"He was a secret agent," I say, even though I'm not sure if that part is true either.

"Yeah, but you can't prove any of what he's saying," Simon insists.

"That's because it's a secret . . . dagnabbit!" I grin.

Simon rolls his eyes. "If you call me a hippie, I'm leaving."

At that moment, we hear voices going past our cabin.

"Who's that?" Josh asks.

"Probably just some kids in the woods." Tyler stretches.

"Dunno." Josh glances at this phone. "It's pretty late, even for the curfew breakers."

We hear muffled guffaws.

"I know who that is," I gasp. "It's Mike and Jake."

"Hold up." Josh pads to the door and opens it a crack, careful not to creak it. We gather around.

"Looks like they're heading toward the lake," Josh whispers.

The moon is out, but the gray clouds scuttling across it make the Rottweilers' movements choppy, like a broken strobe light or like one of those animated flip books that gives the illusion that people are moving. They're pulling something across the grassy clearing, and every so often, there's a clanking sound like something metal hitting rocks.

"Shovels!" I say excitedly. "Maybe they're heading toward the historic site! This must have something to do with Pops and the asteroid. We have to follow them."

"Now?" Tyler says. "There are, like, animals out there."

"Yeah, man, what for?" Josh falls back onto the bed. "I have Rafting for Dummies at the crack of dawn. Yipsy will lose it if I'm late. And Nurse Leibowitz wants me back for my post-shiner checkup."

"This is important," I say, jumping up and grabbing my camera headpiece. "You'll see."

"Wait, Noah." Simon blocks my path. "Now you think the Rottweilers are in on this?"

"Maybe," I answer. "And if they are, I'm going to capture it all on film."

They're all looking at me the way people are usually looking at me. If I had to read their rooms, I'd guess that they're thinking I'm nuts.

"Okay," Simon says resignedly and steps out of my path.

"I'm in too." Tyler throws on his shorts and a tee.

Josh groans but throws on his clothes anyway.

This is awesome! If Earth survives and I've helped, then I can do good, fulfill my Bar Mitzvah project, and—just maybe—get enough awesome film footage so that I can finally go to the DLFC!

CHAPTER 17

We creep through the woods until we hear the dumb-sounding laughs and barks of the Rottweilers.

A few weeks ago, I never would've thought I'd be on a mission to save the world. With friends! Like, real ones who could've picked other friends but chose me.

We find a grouping of bushes where we're covered but still have a good view of Mike and Jake. And they're totally up to something! They've got lanterns, shovels, and a bunch of burlap sacks. They're digging hard—huffing, swigging from water bottles, and spraying dirt everywhere.

"So you really think they're after the same thing your pops is after?" Josh whispers.

"Maybe," I say.

"There must be a connection," remarks Tyler. "I gotta believe they're digging here for a reason."

"To collect artifacts?" Josh suggests.

"Maybe to sell them," Simon says.

We all nod like that explanation feels right.

I'm adjusting my head camera when Mike bends over, and his pants slip way down his behind.

"Butt crack!" Tyler whispers loudly.

"Ugh. Unsee! Unsee!" Josh exclaims, turning away in disgust. He thrusts a stick at me. "Gouge out my eyes!"

Jake's head snaps around like he's an animal who hears prey. He narrows his eyes into the darkness.

"Shh," Simon warns us.

Mike extracts an object from one of the holes.

"What is it?" Simon asks.

I zoom in the lens of my camera.

It's so exciting! The set-up, the lights from the flashlights, and Mike and Jake in action. It's like I'm filming a real movie. Wait till the DLFC people see this!

Mike holds up what looks like a shard of clay. He spits on it and rubs the saliva off with the front of his T-shirt.

"Is it a piece of asteroid?" Simon gently pushes aside some branches for a better view.

"Don't think so." Tyler shakes his head. "Asteroids

are metallic and black. Besides, there really isn't anything astonishing about them. Pieces of asteroid fall to Earth all the time."

We all shoot him a curious look.

"Museum of Natural History," Tyler says. "Field trip."

Mike hands the shard to Jake.

"Whoa, nice," Mike says, turning it over and placing in a satchel by his feet.

"Hey, look." Mike crouches in the dirt, picks up another piece of clay, and brushes the dirt from the front. "This one has some writing on it."

"That'll bring some cash!" Jake grins.

"It's not just about cash, Jake," Mike says, rolling his eyes and his whole head along with them.

"Yeah, yeah," says Jake.

"It's about—"

"Starting our own business," Mike and Jake say at the same time, Mike in an instructive way and Jake like he's sick of hearing it.

"We need money for college, dude," Mike says, slamming his shovel back down into the dirt. "So we can take business classes. Learn marketing and graphs and stuff like that. You can't run a business without knowing that junk."

"For real?" Josh softly barks a laugh. "Business-men. Are they kidding?"

"Well, they *are* selling stuff," Tyler whispers.

"Yeah—try *stealing, then selling*," Josh says.

Mike's phone rings. "Yeah," he answers. "We got more. What? Yeah, well, we are."

Jake stops digging and gestures for Mike to put the phone on speaker. A muffled voice scolds them.

"Who's he talking to?" Josh asks.

"Shh," I rasp, straining to make it out.

Jake and Mike take turns being defensive—talking about how they're doing their best, how they've already found lots of stuff, and how they're sore from this afternoon's activity, Rock Climbing for Klutzes.

They sound nervous and strained, the way other people sound when they're being bullied by *them*.

"Sure, sure." They talk over each other into the phone. "No prob, yeah, sorry, okay, we get it . . ."

"That must be their boss," Simon whispers to Josh.

"We got more," Mike says, looking to Jake for support.

"Tell him, tell him," Jake prompts in a whisper.

"Um, and the piece has writing."

The voice explodes into happy-sounding chatter, causing Jake and Mike to relax.

"Cool, yeah," Jake says.

"We'll have it cleaned off and ready for you to sell," Mike says.

"Yeah, don't worry. No one knows," Jake adds. "We're careful. Yeah."

The voice cuts off, and Mike shoves the phone into his pocket.

"What a jerk," Jake snaps.

"Yeah, well, bosses are jerks." Mike shrugs. "That's why I want to be my own boss."

"Let's go." Mike starts packing up his stuff. "We've got enough for now."

"But what about the thing?"

"What thing?" Josh mouths to us.

"There's no thing," Mike says, swigging his water and packing up his bag. "He's full of it."

"It's pretty big," Jake says. "He'll be pissed if we don't find it."

"So what? Let him find it himself," Mike growls.

"Hey, you ever wondered who he is and what he looks like?" Jake says.

"No," Mike answers. "Don't care. Come on, let's go."

At that moment, there's a loud flapping of bird wings. We all turn our faces to the sky.

"What's that?" Tyler whispers.

"Oh, crud, is that a bat?" Josh ducks.

The wings flap and circle around our heads.

"It's not a bat," I say quietly.

I'd know those flapping bird wings anywhere.

"Shoo, shoo. Not now," I hiss, waving my hands around.

"Is that . . . ? Don't tell me," Simon moans in exasperation.

"Okay," I say, flailing my arms around harder. "I won't."

Mike stiffens, and his head jerks around. "Wait," he says.

"Whatsamatter?" Jake asks, hoisting the duffel over his shoulder. "Come on. Let's go. I need some sleep. I got ceramics tomorrow. Then origami. I'm making a swan ornament for my mom's birthday."

A blur of white and gray swoops lower.

"Is that . . . Sal?" Josh whispers.

"*Coo, coo*," Sal cries.

"Something's out there," Mike says.

"It's just a bird," Jake says, sloping back toward the trail.

Mike shakes his head. "Birds don't fly at night."

"Yeah, well, that one does," Jake snaps.

"*Coo, coo*," Sal warbles and then lands right on my camera headpiece. He lifts his wings, and a gooey mucous-y mess slides down the side of my head.

"Ugh. That is nasty, dude," Josh says.

"Shh," Simon hisses.

"Something's up," Mike repeats. He drops his bag and stomps toward us, his snarling face coming in and out of focus by the swinging light of his lantern.

"*Coo, coo, coo!*" Sal continues to call.

Rotating in small circles, I try to grab for him, but he just keeps hopping around my scalp, his tiny claws sticking into me like needles.

"Come on, Sal," I say. To the others, I add, "He must be nervous."

"Yeah, well, me too! Let's go," Josh urges.

We crouch-run back toward the trail, scrambling and tripping as we go, with Sal bouncing along, clinging fiercely to my camera strap.

"It's dark. I can't see," Tyler whispers urgently.

"This way, I think," Josh says.

"*Coo, coo, coo!*" Sal burbles some more.

"Can't you shut him up?" Simon growls. He makes a grab for Sal, and Sal bites his finger.

"Oww!" Simon snaps his hand back. "That stupid bird bit me."

"You scared him," I say.

"*I* scared *him*?" Simon says.

"Hey!" Mike bellows.

"He's seen us!" Simon exclaims.

"*Coo! Coo!*"

"Jake! Come on! Spies!" Mike yells, and I hear the heavy stomping of boots as the Rotties gallop in our direction.

"Hey! Get back here so we can kill you!" Jake shouts.

"*Coo! Coo!*" Sal is super upset now.

"Ditch the bird!" Josh pants breathlessly as we run and trip and stumble.

"I can't!" I try desperately to grab at Sal. "It's the note! Get the note. He won't leave without delivering it!"

"Well then, you ruddy well better hold still!" Simon dances and darts around me, trying to grab for Sal again.

"I'll try," Tyler says, and he manages to grab hold of Sal.

"The note!" I urge.

"They're over there!" Mike shouts.

"Quick! They're catching up!" I say. "And don't hurt Sal."

Tyler gently cradles Sal, cooing back at him in what sounds like bird language.

And Sal, looking like a dog getting its belly rubbed, vibrates happily in his hands.

"I didn't know you spoke bird," Josh says, fumbling to untie the note.

Tyler shrugs. "At home, every summer, a bunch of them nest in my air conditioner. I talk to them sometimes."

"That's cool," I say.

"That's *weird*." Josh fumbles finally unties the note from Sal's foot. Sal wiggles free from Tyler and flies up toward the moon.

"That way!" Mike gestures to Jake.

"I can't see!" Jake bellows.

"Quick! What does the note say?" Simon asks, sounding panicky.

With shaky hands, I manage to unfold it.

"It says, *Run toward the road*."

The light from Mike's lantern sprays our way, and I can make out the blacktop of the road through the trees. A small flash of light bounces on and off, like some kind of Morse code. We rush toward it and see a small man frantically waving his arms.

"It's Pops!" I yell breathlessly.

A car engine grinds and, through the mist, a large, battered black SUV comes into view.

"Get in! Get in!" Pop shouts, opening the door. We all dive into the back seat, and Pops spryly jumps into the front.

"Step on it, George," he instructs the driver—a short, elderly black guy craning his head to see out the front window. He's wearing coke-bottle glasses, a loud sports shirt, and a cap with tufts of gray hair poking every which-way out from under it.

I whir up the back window just as Mike and Jake, pointing and panting hard, reach the road.

"Don't you hippies have any skills?" Pops explodes. "How are we going to save the world if you get caught?"

CHAPTER 18

"Who are you?" Pops demands, twisting around in the seat, narrowing his eyes at Josh and Tyler.

"Put your seatbelt on, you old coot," George scolds Pops as he chugs up the road at what feels like a cool three miles an hour. A mole crosses our path. George slams on the brakes, and we all jerk forward.

"See that?" George carries on. "You coulda been killed right then. You gotta obey safety rules."

"Keep your pants on," Pops grumbles, fumbling with the seatbelt.

The mole stares into the headlights, his eyes glowing bright red. Slowly, he scuttles across the road, not looking the least bit afraid.

"That's right," George scolds Pops. "You keep on complainin', old man. This isn't your army jeep, swervin' around those narrow German roads. Every time you drove, I said my prayers."

"You're still here, aren't you?" Pops snaps back.

"Well, this isn't 1944 anymore," George says. "It's 2005, and I'm drivin'!"

I lean forward. "Um, actually, it's 20—"

Simon pokes me in the ribs with his elbow, which he can do pretty easily since we're all crushed in the back like a bundle of celery stalks.

George jerks the car to a stop again and swivels all the way around. He's so short that we can only see his glasses through the small gap where the headrest is bolted to the top of the seat. He squints hard, and his eyes almost disappear into his scowling face.

"Now, who is this smart aleck?"

"That's my grandson," Pops says. He leans toward George conspiratorially and whispers loudly, "Don't worry about him. He's a little off."

I'm a little off?!

"Hmph," George grunts. He starts jerking the car up the road again, his foot firmly on the brake.

"Are you trying to loosen my dentures with all that jerky driving?" Pops snaps. "Take your foot off the doggone brake! Or by the time we get to the diner, it'll be tomorrow. These boys are probably hungry, seeing as how it's way past breakfast time already."

Josh, Tyler, Simon, and I exchange confused looks. Outside, it's pitch black, and the clock on the dashboard reads *3:30 a.m.*

"What's going on?" Josh shoots me a sidelong whisper.

"And why are we going to the diner?" Tyler adds.

"In my short acquaintance with Noah's pops," Simon whispers, "I've learned that it's better not to ask questions."

About twenty minutes later, with the pedometer reading that we've traveled about four miles, George slowly pulls into the parking lot of a small, rundown all-night diner. In front is one of those signs encased in little colored bulbs that blink and race around and make you dizzy. The windows glow yellow in the dark, and there are only a few trucks in the parking lot. Through the glass, I see a pair of burly-looking guys eating at the counter.

Simon has been swiping through his texts, but by now, his chin's dropped to his chest, and he's dozed off. Tyler's head is tipped sideways, and a thin line of drool is slipping from the crack of his mouth onto Josh's shoulder. Josh's head is way back onto the seat, his mouth is open, and he's snoring slightly.

But I'm too wired too sleep, and I have too many

questions. It's been such an exciting night. And there's so much spinning around my brain! Are the Rotties really looking for the same thing Pops is? What are they selling, and who's buying it? What is the valuable thing they didn't find? Who were they talking to on the phone?

I remove my headpiece and scratch where the band clutches my scalp. The best part is that I got it all on film!

George pulls into an empty parking spot and keeps adjusting, spinning the steering wheel, jerking us back and forth and back and forth.

Tyler and Josh bump awake.

"Gross, dude!" Josh grimaces, wiping Tyler's spittle off his sleeve.

Simon awakens to the buzzing of his phone, which is practically vibrating off his lap. It looks like he's gotten about a million messages from his mates.

Simon looks around. "Where are we?"

"The diner," I answer.

"Oh, right." He rolls his eyes and stretches his arms above his head. "The diner. Brilliant."

"Your mates are texting," I say.

"Yeah, well, they can wait, can't they?" he says.

"Can they?"

"Sure." A slow grin spreads across his face. "This is way more exciting, right?"

"It is?"

"I mean, I can play football anytime. But how often does a bloke get to save the world with three of his best mates and loopy, geriatric George and Mr. Pops?" He leans across me and peers out the window. "At the Happy Hour Diner, no less. Is there any place else I'd rather be?"

I'm guessing he's being rhetorical and maybe a little sarcastic, so I don't say anything. But I'm happy that he thinks I'm one of his best mates and there's nowhere else he'd rather be.

Pops unclicks his seatbelt and creaks the door open.

"I'm not done parkin' yet!" George growls at him, accidentally leaning on the horn, which blares loudly. Inside the Happy Hour, a trucker angrily raps his knuckles on the window and glares. George whirs his window down and sticks his head out as far as his short neck will allow.

"Have some respect!" he yells. "We fought in the big war. If it hadn't been for us, you'd be eatin' sauerkraut right now!"

"For breakfast? That's nasty," Josh says. "But it's good on hot dogs."

"Agreed." Tyler nods. "But it smells really bad in the refrigerator. My mom has to keep it in a plastic container."

"One that burps?" I ask. "I know all about those!"

"What are you yakking about now?" Pops says. "Get out of the car already!"

"I said," George yells, "I'm not done parkin'!"

"You are now." Pops reaches over and turns the key in the ignition, cutting the engine.

"Time for eggs, pancakes, and coffee," Pops announces. "And time to teach these boys how to save the world."

CHAPTER 19

My body must think it's breakfast time because I'm starving. We order practically everything on the menu and sloppily shovel it in, grunting so loudly that even the truck drivers look disapprovingly at our super-bad manners. The tired-looking waitress, whose name tag says "Madge," keeps bringing stuff. And she's saying things like . . .

"Here you go, hon."

And "You boys are awfully hungry, ain't ya?"

And "What're y'all doing up this early, anyhow?"

Pops winks at us and tells her we're on a fishing trip. Then he and George take turns saying flirty things like . . .

"How come a pretty gal like you's not married?" (Because they asked her if she was married and she said "Not anymore.")

And "I like a modern woman who earns her way."

And "I was a secret agent in World War II, but I'm a lover, not a fighter." (Which is Pops.)

After a while, Madge seems mostly bored and is like, "Uh-huh." And she tells us to pay the cashier.

Outside, the morning glows at the bottom of the hills. I wonder if Nathan has checked our bunk or if Yipsy is doing any nightly rounds. Because even if Nathan wanted to cover for us, if Yipsy saw our empty bunks, he'd freak. Then he'd rat us out to Rabbi Blum, and then Rabbi Blum would call the police, and then the police would call my parents.

I imagine how angry they'd be if they thought I'd just disappeared. Though a small part of me wonders if they'd be just the tiniest bit relieved.

"So, George," I say, draining the last bit of juice from my glass, "are you the same George who was stationed with Pops during the war?"

"One and the same," George says, sipping his coffee from one of those thick, beige-colored ceramic diner mugs.

We all nod silently and keep eating.

"Enough small talk," Pops exclaims. "Now you boys lean in, 'cause I'm gonna explain what's going on."

We lean in.

"First of all . . . who are you?" he demands.

"Um, well, I'm Noah," I start.

"I know who you are!" Pops huffs. "And that's the hippie." He gestures at Simon. "But who are these two?" Pops says, narrowing his eyes. "I hope they're not internet trolls."

Simon coughs like he's trying to hide a laugh.

"Actually, Mr—" Tyler starts.

"Mr. Pops," Simon mouths at him.

"Okay. Well, actually, Mr. Pops," Tyler says, "we're campers. We share a bunk with Noah. I'm Tyler."

"What about you?" Pop snaps at Josh.

"I'm Josh." Josh clears his throat nervously. "You might have caught a glimpse of us the other night in the woods."

"How do I know I can trust you?"

"They just told you, you old coot," George chimes in. "They're friends of your grandson, Ned, here."

"Noah," I say softly, raising my finger in the air.

"Ned, Noah, whatever," Pops says. "You kids think you know everything. Well, let me tell you—"

And suddenly, for some reason—maybe it's all the sugar from the thick shakes, donuts, maple syrup, and pie talking—I kind of feel like I've had enough.

"Pops!" I shout.

A few truck drivers snap their heads around.

"I know you, like, yell at everyone and say things that don't make sense," I say. "But it's getting a little annoying, ya know?"

A hush falls over the table, and all eyes swing toward me. There's no turning back now.

"It's, like, four-thirty in the morning. I'm supposed to be at camp. But I just dragged my new mates into the woods to spy on two big guys digging stuff out of the ground, who are probably gonna beat me up tomorrow. And now I'm in a diner. I don't know what we're doing here. I'm trying to do *tikkun olam*, but I don't even know what this save-the-world business is about! Plus, I'm super tired, and I have Real Boys Swing Dance class first thing in the morning. And if Yipsy finds us missing, we'll probably be sent home. Now could you please tell us what's going on? Oh, and don't call me Ned. Mom and Dad named me Noah. So I'm Noah. Your grandson. Is all that clear?"

It's so quiet you could hear a pin drop, and there's a part of me that's like, *Who just said that?*

But there's another part that feels good. Really good. Like I'm reading this room to the max. I feel more confident than I have in a long time.

Pop stares at me. George puts down his cup and stares at me. Josh lets out a low whistle. Tyler and Simon stare at me, then exchange a *He is so busted* look, darting their eyes everywhere but at me.

Finally, Pops is like, "Who's Yipsy?"

"Gah!" I grunt and drop my head onto the table.

"You tried, mate." Simon pats me on the shoulder.

"Well, do you want to hear what I have to say or not?" Pop says, all exasperated.

"Sure." I lift my head. "Hit me."

"I'm not gonna hit you," Pops replies.

"It was a figure of—"

"It's 4:40," he interrupts, glancing at his watch—one of those big, bubble-faced, magnifying-glass jobs balancing on his skinny wrist.

"That's 0100 hours," George says solemnly.

"Let's get back to headquarters," Pops says.

"And where might that be?" Simon asks.

"The motel! Where else?"

Pops motions for George to slide out of the booth, and his behind makes that squeaky noise across the pleather. Pops slides out after him, and we all follow.

"It's time," Pops announces solemnly, brushing crumbs from his Boy Scout pants, "for you boys to learn the truth."

CHAPTER 20

Fortunately, the motel is only a few blocks from the diner. George pulls into the spot and starts his straightening-the-car routine until Josh is finally like, "Excuse me, sir, but we have to be back at camp by 6:30 at the latest, or Yipsy will go ballistic."

"Again with this Yipsy." Pops throws up his hands. "Saving the world takes time!"

"Don't worry, son." George mercifully cuts the engine, strains to push open the driver's door, and wiggles out. "We'll have you back at camp before breakfast."

Josh and Tyler exchange a look that's like, *I don't think so.*

"I've got a rideshare app," Simon whispers to us. "I can get a car to pick us up in forty-five minutes."

"Good thinking!" Josh says.

The motel is a squat, two-floor building covered with brown shingles. It semicircles around a sad-looking in-ground pool, wavy plastic-and-glass tables, and scattered metallic chairs. A row of identical white doorways stretches across each floor. It's quiet, and most of the curtains are drawn, giving the impression that a lot of rooms are vacant or that people are still fast asleep.

My parents wouldn't want to stay at this motel. If Lily were here, she'd be like, "What. A. Dump!" Then she'd scrunch up her nose like she smelled a skunk.

The night is slowly morphing into lighter shades of gray, and in the distance, the sunlight breaks over the hills. I should be drop-dead tired, but I've bypassed tired and am just super anxious, wondering what Pops and George have to say.

Pops ushers us into his single room, which is a mess. Papers and charts are spread all over the bed and night tables. A whole bunch more are sloppily pasted to the walls. It's a tight fit, and we're all shifting and bumping into each other, unsure of where to stand.

Pops weaves around us, opening drawers and slamming them shut, picking up papers, unfolding them, reading them, and throwing them over his shoulder. The whole time, he's muttering things:

"Dagnabbit!"

And "That's not right."

And "Who put this there?"

I adjust the camera on my head.

"Take that contraption off!" Pops says. "This meeting is top secret!"

"Sorry," I mumble and obediently remove it. But when Pops turns his back, I slip it back on and fluff my hair around it. There's no way I'm not getting this on film. A filmmaker always has to be aware of potential opus moments. And this might definitely be one.

George clears a place for us to sit down.

"Don't move my stuff!" Pop yells at George.

"The boys gotta sit!" George yells back. Suddenly, there's loud pounding on the wall from the room next door.

"Shuddup!" the muffled voice yells. "It's five in the morning!"

George race-shuffles to the wall. "You shuddup! We're tryin' to save the world!"

"No, you shuddup, nut job, or I'll call the manager!" The guy thumps the wall some more.

"Hmph," George grumbles darkly. "Keep it down, kids."

"But we're not—" I start.

"Aha!" Pops exclaims, uncrumpling a ratty newspaper. "Here it is!"

He pins the paper to the wall, grabs a pencil from a drawer, and points to something he's circled in red about a hundred times. "There!"

We all lean in but can't read it because the type is really small.

Tyler takes off his glasses and squints. "It looks like . . . an advertisement for hemorrhoid cream."

"That's not it!" Pops rips the paper from the wall and starts digging through drawers again.

Simon sighs loudly and waggles his phone at me. He's probably already summoned an Uber or a Lyft or something. "Time. To. Go," he mouths.

"Pops." I place my hand on his arm. "Why don't you just tell us what's going on?"

"What's going on . . . is this!" Pops unfolds a chart of the solar system and spreads it out on the bed.

"This is us." He points to the small blue planet, third from the giant sun. "And this is Agatha, the giant black asteroid hurtling toward Earth!"

"Agatha the Asteroid?" Tyler frowns.

"That's right!" Pops waves his pointer finger in the air.

"Seriously?" Josh says.

"Out of the way, you old coot." George shuffles in front of Pops and gently pushes him aside. "Let me explain to these kids. I am part Navajo, after all."

"What does that have to do with—" I start.

"Let him talk." Pops drops into a chair.

George opens a small satchel, pulls out a DVD, pushes a bunch of papers off a laptop, connects some wires, and pushes some buttons.

"Now, don't get any funny ideas about stealin' this DVD." George narrows his eyes at us. "I carry it in this satchel, and I never let it out of my sight."

"What about in the shower?" Josh mumbles.

George spins around looking fiery mad. "You want me to draw you a picture?"

"No, sir," Josh says apologetically to him. Then he's like, "Gross," to us under his breath.

Static buzzes, and a black-and-white image pops up on the laptop screen. A small group of men in army fatigues huddle on cots in some kind of bunker. The image is grainy, and the whole vibe is like a classic movie from the 1940s. And they're saying things I can't quite make out.

The camera focuses on one guy in the middle.

"That's my cousin, Bobby Running Feather," George says proudly. "He's the captain!"

"When was this filmed?" I ask.

"In 1946," Pops says. "Right after the big war. And that's me there." Pops points to a skinny guy sitting next to George's cousin. He looks frighteningly like me—young and earnest with a full head of short, curly hair.

"And that's Sal over there." Pops points to another guy on the screen.

"Hey, the pigeon's namesake!" Josh grins.

"And that's Sammy Swap, 'cause he loved to swap things, and that's Jimmy the Sausage, 'cause he loved sausage. And there's George." Pops points to a younger version of George, still stocky with big glasses and tufts of hair teasing out from under one of those soft army hats.

"I'm the good-lookin' one." George chuckles.

"And that one smoking a cigarette, that was Moe, but we called him Chimney because he was always smokin'."

"Even in his sleep." George shakes his head. "I was always throwing water on him just to keep us from going up in a blaze. Remember that, Mel?"

Pops and George chuckle, then sigh sadly.

"Good men," George says, removing his hat and placing it across his chest. "Good men."

Pops sniffles and wipes his eyes with the back of his hand.

I hate seeing Pops like this. Stepping over all the stuff, I sidle up next to him. "It's all right, Pops," I say, placing my arm around his bony shoulder. "It's okay to be upset. After all, they were your best mates."

"You're a good boy, Ned." He pats my hand and doesn't even pull away.

"Shush now. Here it is." George turns up the remote.

Bobby Running Feather starts talking.

"My cousin was a code talker," George tells us.

"What's a code talker?" Josh asks.

"I know," Tyler says. "I read about it in history. They were Native Americans, specifically Navajos, recruited during World War II. They used the Navajo language to send secret messages that the enemy couldn't decode."

"That's right!" George exclaims. "And my cousin was the best."

"What does that have to do with asteroids?" Josh asks.

"We're getting to that," Pops says, stabbing a bunch of keys on the laptop keyboard. "Dagnabbit, does this get any louder?"

"But here's something I bet you kids didn't know," George says. "Some of these men were working with scientists on a new thing called the space program."

"But the space program didn't start until 1961," Tyler says, and we all turn to him. Is there any obscure fact this kid doesn't know?

"What?" Tyler shrugs a little defensively. "I'm a space nerd."

"Many Native American cultures knew about what we now call astronomy long before white people figured out the world was round," George says.

"Okay, everyone, stop yapping. Here it comes," Pops says, pointing to the screen.

Bobby Running Feather pulls out a map—the same one we're looking at now!

There's also a close shot of a clay tablet covered with some kind of writing. The men are very serious, nodding and saying things that sound like, "Coordinates . . . slam into earth . . . on this tablet . . . hide it . . Levy Homestead . . . this film, for my descendants . . . their responsibility . . . to find . . . to save the world."

The men exchange looks of solemn solidarity. Right afterward, the video goes fuzzy and buzzes out. George carefully removes the DVD and gently places it back in his satchel.

"So . . . what exactly does all of this mean?" I ask.

"The tablet is written in code," Pops shrugs. "That's the point."

"Excuse me," Simon says. "But *what's* the point?"

Pops exhales such a loud huff of exasperation that his whole body goes concave. "That tablet contains a formula to pinpoint the coordinates of the asteroid. Bobby hid the tablet somewhere near the Levy Homestead, and we need to find it to decode the changing coordinates!" He throws his arms up in the air.

"But what about the government?" Tyler asks. "Those guys must already know about this. About the asteroid."

"No, no, no." George pulls his hat back on and shakes his head so hard that it slides over his ear. "No!"

"So . . . that's a no?" Josh quips.

George shoots him a dark look. "Don't be a smart aleck!"

"The government won't listen to us," Pops explains. "For years after the war, we tried to tell those hippie scientists. Just last March, George and I took the Greyhound to Washington . . ."

"That was the bus to Atlantic City," George corrects. "In January, we took the train to Washington."

"Anyways," Pops says. "We tried to tell them. We even showed them the footage."

"And?" Simon asks.

"And nothin'," George says. "They wanted to see the tablet. When we said we don't have it, they treated us like fools. They said there's no Agatha, gave us souvenir mugs, and sent us home."

"That's why we need to find the tablet—to prove it," Pop adds. "Once they see it, they got all kinds of archeology techniques to test it. Authenticate it."

"But Mr. Pops," Simon says gently, "it seems a bit unlikely that NASA and all the other space programs wouldn't know there was a big asteroid hurtling toward Earth."

"I didn't say they didn't know," Pops says, narrowing his eyes slyly. "I said they *said* they didn't know. They don't want us to know they know. Because then we"—Pops makes a huge circle with his arms—"and everyone else will know. Without the tablet, they can dismiss us like we're old kooks."

"I can't imagine why," Josh says softly.

"Think about it, son," George adds. "What do you think would happen if those government people admitted to knowing this? If it got out to the general population?"

"Mass hysteria?" Tyler says.

"Yahtzee," George says, nodding.

"Or maybe," Pops says conspiratorially, "they *want* that asteroid to hit us. Then all the important people can escape in a spaceship, and it won't matter to them if the planet is blown to bits. That's why we need to prove it! Bring it to the people. Force those scientist hippies to destroy Agatha."

"How?" Josh asks.

"They can do it," Pops insists.

"Your pops is right," Tyler says. "I just read something about new technology scientists are using to circumvent and destroy asteroids."

"So is that what the Rottweilers were looking for?" I ask. "The tablet with the secret code?"

"Who? Rottweilers?" Pops says. "You got dogs now?"

"He means those bullies he mentioned before, don't ya?" George asks. "Nah, they're probably just lookin' for antiques to sell to souvenir shops. Happens every year. Some kids figure out they can dig up some wooden spoons and make some change. Nobody can keep 'em off the site."

Outside, the morning is glowing up the place, and crystals of light are dancing off the pool. A car pulls up to the door and idles in the parking spot. Simon's phone pings. We catch eyes. Must be the taxi.

Wow, talk about a confusing room! I want to believe Pops and George and the video. And if the fate of the world is hanging in the balance, then I need to help. This is a serious do-the-right-thing mitzvah moment, after all. But could it really be true?

Outside, a horn blares in short spurts.

"We gotta go," I say as we all start inching toward the door. "It's almost dawn."

"You boys need a lift?" George offers.

"NO!" we shout in unison—a little too enthusiastically.

George's face falls, so I try to soften the blow. "I mean, thanks, but we're good."

We bolt out of the motel door and dive into the taxi. Back to camp and real life. Within seconds, we're swerving onto the main road. Josh and Tyler stare out the windows, looking like they're deep in thought. Simon swipes at what looks like a million texts. Once again, I can't read his room at all.

My thoughts wander to Mia and her song. She's so worried about burping containers destroying humanity, but Earth's destruction might have nothing to do with any of that at all. I'd like to tell her about Ari the Lion and about doing my part to repair the world by trying to stop disaster from striking. I want to show her how I've been capturing it all on film for generations to come. We can talk about how film is a powerful medium after all. I mean, just look how the World War II footage of Pops, George, and Bobby Running Feather reached all the way through time to help us. And wouldn't Nathan be super interested in all this too? Talk about Kabbalah! This here is some serious Jewish mysticism mojo!

I miss Mia and wish I'd asked for her permission before I showed my footage of her. I can only hope she wants to talk to me again.

In the distance, some birds circle the lake, like they've probably been doing since forever. What if we can't save the world? What if we'll really all be gone soon? All that wasted time! All that algebra homework that never mattered after all, all those chores, all that time I worried about not fitting in. And maybe now there'll be no chance to grow up or ever get to DLFC.

I remove my camera and play back all the footage I've taken since heading off to camp. Family. Adventure. Mia. New mates. And now this.

The twisted wire that's sculpted to look like interlocking bread strands—the gate of Camp Challah—comes into view.

Maybe we can prevent the world from being destroyed by Agatha. Maybe this is my chance to really make a difference.

CHAPTER 21

We creep back onto the camp grounds, and it's like we've never been gone. All around us, the daily noises and sights of morning are beginning. Kids are congregating in clumps across the lawns or strolling toward their classes or heading down the embankment to the lake.

Rabbi Blum is giving his morning talk by the flagpole, so we quietly slip into a row by the back. This morning, it's something about a wise rabbi from the Middle Ages and a parable about villages, faith, and livestock. Without Simon interacting and being super interested, the rabbi has been working hard to get a stimulating discussion going.

Fortunately, Simon, now present, asks lots of questions, including why pigs aren't kosher. This gets the rabbi super excited. He waves his travel mug around and launches into a big explanation until his phone erupts in a rousing version of the Maccabeats singing "Dynamite."

Everyone bolts in a dozen different directions.

"Hey, Noah," a voice rings out behind me.

It's Nathan.

Simon, Tyler, Josh, and I exchange guilty and "oh-so-busted" looks.

"Handle it," Simon whispers in my ear before he and my other mates head off toward the mess hall.

"But . . ." I call after them. Too late. I brace myself and swivel around. "Hi, Nathan," I chirp, straining to seem casual.

"So," Nathan says, shoving his book into one of his baggy shorts pockets, "I checked in on you guys a couple of times last night, and you weren't there."

"Yeah, about that . . ." I start, my mouth tugging in all directions. It's so hard to make your face look like you're not lying when you're just about to. Especially when you keep lying to the same guy. "Sorry. We were, um . . . Are we in trouble?"

Nathan stares at me hard for a few seconds. I cannot read his room at all.

"Nah," he finally says. "But I would like to know what you were doing."

Janine and Sarah slide by, both looking cheery in the tie-dyed shirts they probably made in Not Your Mother's Tie-Dye. Janine's long blond braids swat at her shoulders as she moves.

"Hey, Nathan," she says, smiling. "We'll all be at the lake after dinner if you want to join."

A burst of bright crimson blooms at the base of his neck and creeps slowly into his face, and he works up a smile that looks more like a grimace. He sort of nods, then sort of stops until his face goes slack.

"Oookaay." Janine draws out the word and knits her brows. "Well, we'll be there."

"Ahikejk," Nathan mutters. He holds up his palm in a wave, then awkwardly slams it against his chest like he's doing the Pledge of Allegiance.

Sarah breaks into a giggle, and she and Janine rush off, Janine's braids flapping behind her.

"What did you just say?" I ask.

"I—I don't know," Nathan says, looking mortified.

"Do you want me to teach you about girls?" I say, leaning in confidentially. "I mean, I'm no expert, but I think I've got a handle on the basics."

Nathan looks crestfallen.

"Well, for one," I say, "you have to speak English. And don't do that thing with your hand."

"Yeah, well, back to you." Nathan straightens and clears his throat. "Just tell me where you guys were and what you were doing, okay?"

Should I tell him? No. Probably not. Better to go with a half-truth.

"I was researching my Bar Mitzvah project about saving the world," I say, "and my mates were helping me. Then we took a walk around camp. Then we sat down and rested. Then we talked some more. Then we dozed off over there in the pine needles. Then we hit the outhouse. Then we—"

"Got it," Nathan interrupts, holding up his palms. "At any rate, I'm glad you were working on your project. We can talk about it later if you like. Maybe after the last activity, before dinner, or—"

"Pssst, come on!" Tyler pokes his head out of the mess hall door, saving the day.

"Um, I'll let you know," I say to Nathan. "Gotta go!"

"Sure," he calls out after me. "Just no more all-nighters, 'kay?"

"No problem!" I swing through the screen doors.

Of course, I shouldn't have made that promise. But it really won't be a problem if Agatha the asteroid blasts the planet to bits.

"Didn't we just eat?" I ask, jumping into the food line behind Simon.

"That was hours ago," he responds. "Besides, that meal threw off my internal clock. Gotta reset. How'd it go with Nathan?"

"Fine. I told him I was working on my Bar Mitzvah project and you guys were helping. I was vague."

"You mean you lied?" Josh grins.

"Well, for his own safety." I frown. "You think that's bad?"

"I'm just messin' with you!" Josh punches my arm. "It's cool. The truth would just get him upset."

"Yeah, sometimes lying is the best option," Tyler adds solemnly. "A famous Talmudic scholar once said you have to be cruel to be kind."

"Really?" Simon cocks his head. "Was it Rabbi Akiva from the first century?"

"No." Tyler rolls his eyes. "I'm kidding. It's a song from the eighties." He hums out the tune as we slide down the food line with our trays.

"This might sound ridiculous," Josh remarks, "but I'm too tired to be tired."

"I know what you mean," Tyler agrees.

"Actually," Simon adds, "now I'm staaaaarving."

"Look, it's pancake day!" Josh says brightly.

"Pancakes and maple syrup." Simon looks dreamy. "Lovely."

"Lovely?" Josh echoes. "Dude, you need to Americanize your vocabulary."

Simon flips him a universal gesture. "American enough for you?" he says.

"Now you're gettin' it." Josh grins.

"Hurry up before everyone scarfs up the chocolate chip ones," Tyler says.

I stop dead in my tracks. Could they really have forgotten about saving the world?

"Come along, Noah," Simon says crisply, as they pile up their plates.

My eyes sweep the room, but I don't see Mia—just her friends at their usual table, laughing and yakking.

"Aren't you guys worried about, ya know, the world?" I ask them quietly.

"What about it?" Josh says, popping a hash brown into his mouth.

"Are you kidding?!" I say.

"This way," Simon says, catching Lily's eye and gesturing for us to sit with her and her friends.

The Rottweilers enter the mess hall. I keep my head down and pick up my pace, bumping right into Tyler's back.

"Hey, watch it, Noah," he says.

"It's Mike and Jake," I whisper hoarsely into his shoulder.

"So what?" Josh throws his leg over the bench.

"Good morning, ladies," Simon says coolly as he slides in next to Lily.

"Hey, Simon." Lily tilts her head, tucks a stray hair behind her ear, and gives me a dark look.

"Your hair is like, everywhere, Noah. Could you at least try and look normal?" she says.

"Sorry, Lily. I was just up all night trying to save the world from a killer asteroid."

"And, once again, I'm sorry I'm even talking to you," she says, pivoting her body toward Simon.

"Snaps from my mates," Simon says to Lily, showing her his phone. "Want to see?"

How can they all be acting like nothing is wrong?

"Nice action shots," Lily notes.

"Yeah, nice," I say, wiggling my eyebrows in Simon's direction. "Especially since Earth and everyone on it is going to die soon."

"He means . . . it's a death match. Football—er, *soccer* death match." Simon arches his eyebrow at me.

"Shouldn't we be talking about the thing?" I persist.

"What thing?" Josh says, spraying me with bits of pancake.

"You don't really believe all that stuff, do you?" Tyler asks.

"Well . . . yes," I say. "I think I do."

"It's just two lonely old guys," Josh says, taking a swig of juice, "making up stuff for attention. Happens all the time."

"It does?"

"Sure," Tyler says. "It's like when an old lady calls the cops because she thinks there's a burglar, but there isn't one."

"Yeah." Josh nods. "A couple of months ago, my neighbor Mrs. Goldstein, who's like a hundred, called the fire department because her cat, Waffles, was up a tree. Then she made those guys hang around and drink iced tea for, like, an hour."

"Simon?" I say. "You believe it, don't you?"

"Um, not really," he says over Lily's head.

"What?!" I blurt out. "What about everything we just saw and heard? What about the video and"— I lean in—"the Rottweilers?"

"Well, yeah, they're jerks and thieves, but that's life." Josh downs the rest of his juice, crumbles his napkins, and chucks them onto his tray.

"So that's it?" I ask in disbelief. "You're not gonna do anything about it?"

"Sorry, dude," Josh says as he and Tyler get up to leave. "Not that civic-minded. Besides, it's time for canoeing."

"I've got archery," Tyler says.

"I've got Advanced Anatomy for Future Surgeons." Simon lifts his tray as Lily and her friends also stand to go.

"But, but—" I stammer as they move around me.

"See you later, mate." Simon pats my back.

I can't believe my ears. Doesn't anyone care about saving the world?

As if on cue, Mia slides through the door. Aha! Now, talk about someone who's civic-minded! Talk about someone who cares about the world!

Mia smiles at Trina, Marisa, and Jyll and heads their way. Jyll's eyes slide up at her, but she doesn't smile or wave. She just scowls before leaning back toward her friends.

Looking like she's been slapped, Mia stops dead, then veers away to sit at a corner table by herself. She stirs her oatmeal but doesn't even eat it, glancing up every few seconds to steal a glance at the girls. Finally, Mia's face crumbles, and she rushes from the mess hall. I rush out after her.

Adjusting my eyes to the bright morning sun, I catch flashes of her black boots weaving through the brush, cutting across the camp grounds toward the trail leading to the homestead site.

"Mia!" I call out and take off after her—across the lawn, past the volleyball court, and onto the dirt trail. "Mia!"

Suddenly, a meaty hand grips my arm hard and jerks me back.

"You!" Jake Rottweiler snarls into my face. "You're just the guy I was looking for."

"Me?" I squeak.

"I wanna talk to you," he says.

"Oh, well, great! I'd love that," I blather. "But, oh, look at the time."

I glance at my watchless wrist. "I'm late for Mosaic Art for Budding Chagalls. Then I gotta sprint down to the boathouse for Midmorning Tai Chi and—Help!" I blurt at some kids rushing toward the lake.

"Shut up," Jake growls, dragging me farther down the wooded path.

Scraggly branches scratch my arms and legs, and my frightened breath is quick and shallow. My life flashes before my eyes: the porpoise aquarium with Bailey and Rex, Pops's paranoid ramblings at his birthday party, Mom, Dad, Lily, camp, mates . . . Next, my mind wanders to the life I may never have: a date with Mia at a karaoke club, getting a standing ovation for my short opus at the DLFC, schmoozing with Hollywood players, winning an Oscar. Lily, in the audience, clapping proudly, saying, "That's my brother." Dad saying that if he could have chosen any son in the world, it would have been me! Images of me somehow saving the world. Doing lots and lots of *tikkun olam*. Being a Jewish hero like Moses.

No, no, I think wildly. *Life can't end like this!*

"Where are we going?" I sputter. "Can't we talk about this? If you let me live, I won't tell anyone about your stealing and potentially interfering with saving humanity as we know it."

"WHAT?" Jake snaps.

"I'm sorry, I meant to say—I won't rat you out about your business endeavor, even though it's kind of illegal. Please don't kill me. Or hurt me a lot."

"Shuddup!" he barks.

We reach a small clearing near a burnt-out campfire. Mike Rottweiler is there, leaning against a tree, chewing on a long stalk of grass.

Jake throws me down. The grainy dirt scrapes my knees and the palms of my hands.

"Get up," Mike commands.

Slowly, I pull myself to my feet. Trying to be inconspicuous, I reach into my backpack. If only I could turn on my camera or phone.

Mike smacks my arm. "No camera, geek."

"Yeah, don't even think about it," Jake chimes in.

"People will be looking for me," I croak.

"Who?" Mike taunts.

"My mates," I say.

"Pffft!" Jake snorts a laugh. "Yeah, right."

"And, um, my pops. And my sister, Lily . . . well, maybe not Lily. But Rabbi Blum and Nathan and Yipsy, once they notice I'm gone. Eventually my parents, my teachers, the police—who'll probably put out an Amber Alert—and Channel 12 news and maybe the mayor. He's good friends with my uncle Larry. George, the old folks at Shady Pines . . . although they don't really go outside much, but they have cell phones and can make plenty of calls. My—"

"Will you SHUT UP!" Jake shouts, up in my face.

We stare at each other for what seems like forever. I wish I knew what they were thinking! Please, God, if I ever I needed help reading a room, it's now.

"So . . ." I try, "how do you like camp?"

"Stop talking!" Mike groans.

"Whadda we do with him?" Jake says.

"Is that rhetorical?" I ask. "Because, if not, you could just let me go so—"

"Shuddup," Mike barks yet again. "What did you bring him here for?"

"You told me to!" says Jake.

While they bicker, I inch away toward the trees. If I could just get to that grouping of pines, I could sprint my way back to the lake and civilization.

Jake grabs my arm. "You're not going anywhere," he growls.

"Let's just tell 'im," Mike squints his eyes menacingly at me. "And then I'll punch him or something so he knows we're serious."

"You can just tell me," I say. "No punching is necessary."

Jake pins my arms while Mike moves so close to my face that I can count the pimples on his forehead. There are twelve. Plus two whiteheads and a pockmark scar where he must have scratched a pimple too hard.

"Listen," Mike says. "What you saw and heard the other night. You didn't see or hear it. Got it?"

"Sure," I say.

He steps back.

"Is that it?"

"You want more?" Mike growls, pushing in even closer so that now I can count the underdeveloped hair bristles on his upper lip. There are seven.

"No, no," I say. "I'm good."

"Great." Jake nods to Mike. "Now punch him out. Make it bloody."

Mike pulls his fist back.

"Wait, wait!" I cower. "I just wanna know, before I'm supposed to forget, the valuable thing you were looking for. What is it?"

"None of your beeswax!" Jake yells.

"You don't know, do you?"

"Duh, of course we know," Mike snaps.

"Because it's pretty special," I say.

"Whaddaya mean?" Mike squints quizzically.

"Will you punch this guy already?" Jake huffs.

"Wait! Wait," I beg. "It's just that I bet you're not getting enough money for it. I bet your boss is ripping you off."

"Pffftt," Mike snorts. "Well, I been sayin' that since fourth grade."

Fourth grade?

"I could give you lots more money for it," I say. "Lots."

"Yeah?" Mike narrows his eyes. "Where would you get lots of money?"

"I have a very rich contact," I answer. "Just let me go, and I'll contact my contact, and my contact can be your contact, and you'll make a contact that will be worth your while. Who is *your* contact, by the way?"

"Huh?" Mike says.

"He's lying," Jake says. "Just beat him up so he knows not to mess with us anymore. So he knows he'll get it worse if he squeals."

"I'm not lying," I say. "I swear. What you're looking for could save your life and the lives of everyone you know, including all your friends—if you have any, which I doubt. But you could be on the news."

"Which channel?" Mike asks.

"All. All of the channels," I say. "And cable and Netflix and Hulu and Amazon Prime."

"Okay, Turtle," Mike says skeptically. "What is this thing that's gonna make me a hero and get me on the news?"

"It's . . . it's a secret code," I say slowly. "About Agatha the asteroid."

"Oh for . . ." Jake says. "Mike, just beat him up

already. I got Virtual Reality Space Travel to Israel in five minutes."

"It's true, I swear!" I insist. "I could explain it better if you weren't squeezing my forearm and cutting off the blood supply to my brain."

Jake loosens his grip, and I break for the woods. But Mike jumps into my path. He grabs me and yanks me hard by my shirt collar.

"OW, OW, OW!" I yell.

"I haven't even hit you yet," Mike says, pulling back his fist. "You ready?" He grins sadistically, aiming right for my eye.

"Not the face!" I yell. "A filmmaker's eyes are his windows to the world!"

He moves his fist to the right.

"Not the shoulder! That's where I balance my camera!"

He aims lower.

"Not the stomach! I'm lactose intolerant!"

He smirks and aims way down.

"Oh, no! Definitely no! No, not there!" I plead.

Mike rolls his eyes, pulls his fist back, and aims straight for my nose.

"OWWWWWW!" I scream and twist my head before he even makes contact.

"Help me hold him, Jake," Mike commands.

I wonder what could make someone enjoy this so much.

"You must be very unhappy to enjoy hurting me," I say. "But you know, the sign in Rabbi Blum's office says, *Only Hashem Can Heal All Wounds!*"

"Do it!" Jake grunts, struggling against my struggling.

"Okay, do it!" I yell. "But you won't stop me from saving the world!"

Mike screws up his face and tightens his fist, pulling it way, way back. I brace for contact.

"OWWWWW!!!!" I howl again, preemptively.

"Leave him alone!" a voice booms from behind the trees.

We all turn to see Mia, standing by the edge of the trail, holding a large forked branch in her hands.

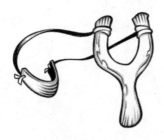

CHAPTER 22

"Ha! Whaddaya gonna do?" Mike says.

"Yeah, you gonna sing us some dumb song about peeeace and looove?" Jake draws out the words, following them up with loud kissing sounds.

On cue, Mia does indeed break into song in her low, warbly style. It's something about peace, love, toxic car emissions, and slingshots.

And while Mike and Jake stare, like, totally perplexed and confused, Mia lifts the forked branch, fits a small rock against the thick rubber band stretched across it, takes aim, and shoots. A rock whizzes past Jake's ear at lightning speed.

"Hey!" Jake winces, cupping his head. He releases his grip on me, and I bound over to Mia, who reloads with another rock.

"Next time," she announces, "I won't miss."

Stunned and wide-eyed, Mike and Jake bolt.

"Come on!" I grab Mia's arm, and we run the other way, panting and stumbling as we go, not looking back to see if the Rottweilers following us until we're all the way at the far side of the lake.

In the distance, dozens of kids and counselors are gathered, happily swimming and paddling canoes. I spot Josh, Tyler, and Simon goofing around, playing Star Wars lightsabers with some oars until Yipsy steps in, directing them to a group doing the slow dance of Tai Chi.

"Hey!" I wave, trying to catch Simon's eye.

"Wait!" Mia pulls me back behind the trees. "Aren't you forgetting something?"

"Oh. Um. I guess I forgot to say thanks," I say awkwardly. I reach for her hand and give it a few hearty shakes. "You saved the day back there."

"Um, yeah." She jerks her hand back, wiping it on her shorts. "That's not what I meant."

"Um . . . I liked your song?" I try.

"And?" she prompts.

"And your really superior slingshot work."

"And?" she repeats and waits.

Suddenly, I'm embarrassed to talk to her—to tell her about Pops, Agatha, saving the world, and how she and Moses are my role models for doing *tikkun olam*.

It was so way easier when I talked to Mia in my daydreams. I was suave and not awkward. The words flowed, and sometimes I even had a British accent like Simon. I made clever jokes and she laughed. And I was wearing cool boots—okay, so that part was weird, but it made me feel confident.

"Noah!" Mia snaps her fingers in front of my face. "You there?"

"Oh, sorry," I say. "I was just . . . thinking."

"Yeah, well, maybe you could do that later. I'm kind of late for Glass Blowin' in the Wind. What was that all about anyway? How did you end up alone in the woods with those bullies?"

But before I can even answer, her face darkens, and she looks away. "Forget it. I really shouldn't even be talking to you."

And all of a sudden, her room is really confusing, and I don't even know where to begin. Is she still mad at me from the other day when she saw herself singing on the big screen during Show Your Stuff? I think she is. I'm sure it just didn't match up with the daydream she has of herself.

"Sometimes," I say, "we don't see ourselves like the camera sees us."

"Huh?"

"The camera," I repeat. "It's the way the world see us. 'Cause the way we are in our heads kind of distorts how we are. Sometimes in good ways, sometimes in bad."

Mia chews the inside of her cheek, and her eyes swing over and settle squarely onto mine.

"So I'm sorry if I distorted your head image," I continue, "but I think you looked awesome on the screen during Show Your Stuff. And, like, that's how I see you. Different."

"Yeah, right," she says bitterly, picking up a dead leaf and shredding it. "Different. That's code for *weird*."

"No way," I say. "You're different in a good way. You don't need to change the letters of your name to seem special. You *are* special."

She tilts her face to mine. "Yeah?" A tiny smile tugs at her lips.

"Like, people don't get me sometimes," I add, "but I'm kind of learning that the people who do get me are my real mates."

How have I not noticed the green and amber flecks in her brown eyes until now?

"And you really care about things." I'm on a roll. "Important things like toxic car emissions and plastic burp-y containers and the spiritual importance of the moon in connection with lady parts."

We're leaning in close now, and it feels like I'm really reading her room and we're connecting and I wish I was filming this for my opus, 'cause it's even better than my daydream.

"I do care about those things." She nods. "I really do."

"And that's, like, awesome," I say.

"Want to know something?" she asks quietly.

I don't answer. So far I've counted five green flecks around her irises.

"Well, do you?" she persists.

"Sorry, I thought you were being rhetorical."

"I don't even like Trina or Marisa or Jyll," she confides.

"Then why do you try to so hard to get them to like you?"

"You noticed that?" she says, her eyes widening in surprise. "You're, like, perceptive."

Someone thinks I'm perceptive? That's a first!

"It's just like . . ." She shrugs, twisting one of her earrings and looking far away. "At home, I'm the school weirdo and I'm okay with that. It sort of gives me, like, an identity. But sometimes I think about what it would be like to be cool, go to parties, have friends to text, have a boyfriend . . ." A slight pink blush crawls up her cheeks, and she slides her eyes to mine. "But the more I pretend to be like my bunkmates, the less they like me. That makes me feel all off balance and hurt, and I was starting to forget who I really am. Is that dumb?"

I'm not sure because I'm distracted by how cute she looks and how her fingers wave around while she talks and how the dappled sun glints off her hair. Also, I'm super hungry, and I'm not really following what she's saying.

"Yes?" I try, hoping that's the right answer.

"Hey, ya know, I should turn all my feelings into a song," she says, brightening. "It could be about social conscience vis-à-vis identity. Whaddaya think?"

"It also has great cinematic potential," I say. "Like a memoir opus with music."

As if on cue, my stomach makes a low, growly musical noise.

"Yeah, me too." She gestures to my stomach. "Let's get lunch. We'll see what's organic."

I'm more in the mood for a hamburger than a plate of kale and carrot frizzies, but I'm feeling super excited because . . . is this a date?!

We start back up the path—until she stops and grabs my arm.

"But," she says seriously, "I still wanna know what was going on back there. With Jake and Mike."

So now I'm stuck because I know that she's not being rhetorical. Am I ready to tell her?

At that moment, a pigeon swoops low on a branch, glares at me, and coos.

"Later, Sal," I call and wave him away.

Mia shoots me a curious look as we climb out of the woods toward the mess hall.

CHAPTER 23

"Wow!" Mia exclaims, wiping the salad dressing dribbling down her chin.

"So you believe me?" I ask.

I've told her everything.

"Well, sure!" she blurts enthusiastically. "I mean, life is full of unbelievable stuff. Funny, though—I've spent the last few years spreading the word about saving the planet from selfish consumerism and waste. But the real killer might just be some random asteroid from space named Agatha. That's heady!"

"Mmmm." I nod.

"But, like, it's also kind of spiritual," she says earnestly. "Like the universe is fed up with us or something. Like we're being punished for being bad guardians of Mother Earth."

"You think God is punishing us?" I ask.

"Maybe She is," Mia says. "Or maybe punishment is a harsh word. Maybe She's just trying to teach us something."

"That's not really fair if we get squashed before we get a chance to learn," I say. "I think it's kind of a test. According to Ari the Lion from the sixteenth century and Nathan Blum—well—now, God wants us to fix the world. That's what we're wired to do. And the world gets better when you do good things, 'cause the good things bring light. And the light snuffs out the dark, dark being evil. And then there's a bunch of mystical stuff that's involved, but I'm not clear on that part."

Mia nods pensively.

"And light is what the world needs," I finish with a flourish.

"I thought it was love," Mia says. "All the major poets and lyricists talk about the world needing love."

"I guess that works too." I shrug.

Mia leans back in her seat, cocks her head, and stares at me. I can't read her expression at all, which makes me anxious. I wonder if there's something hanging out of my nose or she's thinking she doesn't like me anymore.

"So what's the plan?" she says, slurping her pear juice. "You're gonna need one, you know."

I don't know what to say but, fortunately, it's about noon and everyone's filing in.

Simon, Tyler and Josh head my way, but when they catch sight of us, they hesitate. I wave them over.

"Hi, Mia," Simon says, sliding into the seat and grinning at me over her head. Tyler and Josh sit down too, and we're all kind of uncomfortable.

"Mia knows," I say.

"Oh," Tyler blurts, surprised.

"Um," Josh says, "weren't we gonna, like, keep this to ourselves?"

"Boys club much?" Mia cocks her eyebrow. "You need some female empowerment energy here."

They exchange annoyed glances. "What makes you think that?" Josh asks, chewing loudly on a piece tofurky bacon.

"It's obvious," she says. "You don't have a plan."

"We've got a plan," Simon says. "Or . . . we will."

"Really?" Mia presses, unconvinced.

Simon shifts uncertainly.

This isn't going well. I need to draw on the team-building skills I learned from Mrs. Burns, the school social worker, by introducing a common goal or, in this case, a common enemy.

"She saved me from the Rottweilers," I announce.

"Mike and Jake?" Simon glances up from his plate. "What happened?"

"They know we're onto them. They dragged me into the woods. They were gonna beat me up."

"Don't tell me," Josh says around a mouthful of food, looking disbelieving. "Mia scared them off with one of her songs." Josh holds up his palms and pretends to be afraid. "Ahh! Don't sing to me! I'll do anything!"

Tyler and Simon guffaw.

"So not funny," Mia says.

At that moment, Jyll & Co. glide past.

"Well now, *that* makes sense," Jyll sneers at Mia.

"Yes, it does," Mia says loudly, shooting her a sunny smile.

Jyll looks surprised for a second before she gets all snide again. The three of them click their sandals to the other side of the room.

"Guys," I say, "you don't understand. Mia's incredible with a slingshot."

Simon stops just before the fork hits his mouth, and Tyler's expression shifts to interested.

"A slingshot?" Josh says. "What is this, the 1950s? Did you bring Lassie too?"

"You gotta see it," I insist.

"Afraid?" Mia narrows her eyes at Josh.

"Yeah, right!"

"Free period's next. You're on." Mia glares at him, crumples her napkin, and chucks it onto her plate. "You and me. Behind the outhouses."

"Way behind," Tyler suggests, gagging.

"Let's go!" I smile.

Mia, Tyler, and Josh slide out the door, but I bump straight into Lily. Her gaze swings over to Mia.

"Where are you all going?" she asks suspiciously. "And why didn't I see you at the campfire last night?"

"Hi, Lily!" Simon steps between us. "Don't you look nice today!"

"Covered in gray muck from the potter's wheel? I seriously don't think so," Lily replies, stepping around him. "What are you up to, Noah?"

"Nothing." I swallow hard.

"Hmm," Lily says. "Not convinced."

"Don't worry. He'll stay out of trouble. I'll watch him." Simon winks and throws his arm around my shoulder.

"Uh-huh," Lily says. "And who's gonna watch you?"

"How about you?" Simon leans in, all charming.

A soft pink blush crawls up Lily's cheeks. She quickly flips her hair and pretends she's not flattered, then leans in to me so close that our eyeballs are almost touching.

"Just," she says. "Don't. Embarrass. Me."

CHAPTER 24

Crack!

The rock hits a corner of the outhouse, chipping off a tiny piece of shingle.

"No way!" Josh exclaims. "I had that shot!"

"You need to feel the trajectory of the rock," Mia instructs. "Like, in your breath, in your chest."

Mia aims for the back of the door and lets her rock fly. It pings loudly and hits right in the center, making a large mark. "See?" she says.

"Hey!" a voice yells from inside. "Cut it out!"

"Got it." Josh nods solemnly. "Breathe. Aim."

Chris from Bunk 3 stumbles from the outhouse, tucking his shirt into his shorts. "You mind?!" He scowls at us as he stomps off.

"I thought you checked to see if it was empty," Tyler says to Josh.

"No, dude. I only go in there when absolutely necessary," Josh answers. "I thought *you* checked."

This will make awesome footage for my opus, I think happily as I adjust my camera headpiece. My mates and me, horsing around, damaging camp property, strategizing to save the world.

"Can I have a go?" Simon reaches for the slingshot.

Mia gives him a quick overview of slingshot placement—explaining something about aim, velocity, cleansing meditative breaths, and letting it fly. Which he does.

"Yes!" Simon pumps his fist in the air. "A perfect shot."

"Not bad," Mia says reluctantly.

"He plays soccer," I announce, proud that my best mate and my potential girlfriend are bonding over sports.

"It's not exactly the sa—" Simon pauses mid-syllable. "Never mind."

"Free period's almost over," Tyler says, checking his phone. "We better come up with a plan."

Mia and I sit on flat rocks, and Simon and Tyler sit on the ground, making a circle.

"So . . . um . . . what do we do?" Tyler says.

"I dunno," I reply. "But we have to move fast. According to our sources, Agatha is set to strike within weeks. That means Pops and George have to get the tablet, get to Washington, show the government the tablet, convince the government that they're ready to go public, and give the government enough time to destroy the asteroid. That's a lot."

"How are we gonna find the tablet?" Mia asks.

"I bet Mike and Jake know where it is," I reply.

"So we follow them and, hopefully, they'll lead us to it," Simon suggests.

"What if they don't?" Tyler asks.

We ponder this for a second.

"Then we're in trouble," I say.

We all agree to that.

In the distance, Yipsy's whistle blows.

"So, step one," Simon says, "we follow Jake and Mike. Tyler, Josh, Noah, and I will slip out after dinner."

"Wait," Tyler interrupts. "It's Hangout Thursday. Nathan will probably notice if we don't show up."

"We can meet here then," I say. "Afterward."

"No, too much traffic by the outhouse," Josh says.

"What about over there where the path ends?"

Mia suggests. "Past the signpost, a few yards down the embankment."

Yipsy's whistle blows sharply again.

"Right." Simon nods.

"I'll send a Sal note to Pops and George," I say.

"It's on!" Josh and Tyler slap hands.

As the guys head for the bunks, Mia grabs my sleeve. "I just wanted to say thanks."

I turn to her. "For what?"

"For, like, including me," she says. "And for reminding me about stuff . . . that, like, I care about."

She takes a step toward me. She's closer than she's ever been. She smells a little like guitar-string resin. I know this because my friend Bailey from film club plays the cello.

It's already a hot day, and here in the woods, the morning dew mists and sizzles off the flat green leaves, causing me to wonder, what do I smell like? Are my armpits rank? Also, what's tickling my ankle? I fight the urge to lean down and scratch it.

Is Mia about to kiss me? If so, I really regret not brushing my teeth for, like, four days.

"So, um," Mia continues, "I hope we can, like, save the world. It's a really timely cause and not even overexposed like other causes. We could totally spearhead the movement. I could write penetrating songs, and you could make meaningful films. It could be like the '60s, but with social media."

She steps in closer. "But if we don't save the world in time, we could, like, die soon."

"Yeah," I say.

And, wow, I'm super nervous.

"Have you ever kissed anyone?" she asks, leaning in so close that I can count the small pores in her nose. There're more than twenty.

I don't know if I know how to kiss, and that thing tickling my leg just bit me. I reach for my ankle just as she dives in, and our heads smack together.

"OW!" we both exclaim at once.

Then there's just a lot of talking over each other like, "Sorry, sorry!" "No, sorry." "It's all right. Are you all right?" "Yeah, yeah. You?" "Yeah. You?" "Fine." "You sure?"

Yipsy's whistle shrieks long and loud. Last call.

It's super awkward for a few seconds. I readjust my headpiece, and she looks all embarrassed. Eventually, she tucks her hair behind her ear, clears her throat, and jumps in front of me onto the path. I scramble up behind her.

Wow! Saving the world and almost getting my first kiss! I guess coming to Camp C was the right thing to do after all, because I can't imagine that the DLFC could be any more exciting than this!

Tyler, Simon, Josh, and I slip back to the bunks. After a few hours' sleep, all I can do is lie awake and think about our plan. Or more specifically, all the holes in our plan.

What if Mike and Jake have no idea where the tablet is? What if they do but don't want to give it to us? What if their contact is a big angry guy with no neck who wears a trench coat and wants to whack us? What if, by the time George drives his usual three-miles-an-hour over to the camp and spends another ten minutes parking the car, we've already been whacked? What if squatting in the woods results in me getting tick bites in places I don't want the doctor to examine?

The rest of the day is like being in some moody film-noir Hitchcock movie, moving through camp in slo-mo, nodding to friends and acquaintances and catching the eyes of all the main players.

On the way to Virtual Bungee Jumping, Tyler, Simon, and I share a secretive look.

In Armchair Travel to the Precambrian Age,

I shoot Josh a sly thumbs-up, and he winks.

Strolling past the baseball field, where I almost get hit by a rogue ball, Mia and I exchange shy nods.

During CPR for Future Doctors, I spy the Rottweilers swinging over the lake on tire swings. They narrow their eyes angrily at me before belly-flopping into the lake.

And throughout the day, I repeatedly pass Lily and her friends, and she pretends not to see me. But by the fourth time, her bro-dar kicks in. She glares directly into my face. She knows something's up.

I think I'll miss her.

CHAPTER 25

It's about an hour before Operation Save the World, and I realize I have no way of contacting Sal. So I decide to call Pops on his phone. Then it's about fifteen minutes of him hanging up on me by accident, re-dialing, dropping the call, and shouting "Dagnabbit!" into the receiver.

I finally text him: *Send Sal.*

He answers with a garbled, super long text followed by about twenty ridiculous emoticons that make no sense at all.

By now, it's time for Hangout Thursday. Kids amble in from all corners of camp, following the awesome smell of barbecue like it's a long smoky finger from a cartoon beckoning them toward the festivities on the great lawn.

I stand at the edge of the tetherball court, trying

to look inconspicuous, and turn slowly so that my camera headpiece can catch the 360-degree mood of the scene. It's a dusky twilight, and everyone's laughing, eating, and horsing around. The counselors are lighting fire pits and tiki torches as music blares.

Yipsy's sitting with Nurse Leibowitz, sloppily eating roasted potatoes. Nurse Leibowitz is slurping soup and squinting into the crowd like she's just waiting for someone to choke or fall or get bitten by something that requires emergency EpiPen intervention.

All around, friendships are being forged, and I wonder: Will some kids be friends for life? Will some come back year after year and then become counselors and then become Yipsys? Will my friendships with my mates last? I sure hope so.

Suddenly, I feel sentimental about camp, even though I'm still here. In my mind, I flash forward to months from now, when I'll be staring out the window in algebra, thinking back on just this moment. I know I'll miss camp a lot.

The sky darkens as I slip away to the designated meet-up spot. Behind me, the sounds and sights of camp life fade.

"Hey, pssst!"

I startle as Simon comes up behind me.

"Hey," I say softly. "Let's go."

"Um, about that," Simon says, his eyes darting away from mine. "I sort of have, um, something I have to do."

"Whaddaya mean?" I ask, feeling uneasy at the bottom of my stomach.

"Well, ya see, some of my mates are having their big match, and it's in real time, in just about two minutes." He checks his phone. "And I really need to see it."

"Can't somebody record it so you can watch it later?"

"No!" Simon shakes his head emphatically.

"Well . . . can't you miss it?" I try. "This is kind of important."

"My mates back home are counting on me," Simon says defensively.

"But *we're* counting on you to help save the world!" I remind him, getting a little angry now.

"Noah," Simon says, checking his phone again, "all this has been fun to play at, but—well—you know this isn't real."

"Whaddaya mean?"

"I mean, it's been cool to talk about saving the world and such, but it's all . . . rubbish," he says.

"Whaddaya mean?'

"Stop saying *whaddaya mean*!" Simon snaps.

"You don't believe it?" I say, incredulous. "How can you say that? We have proof."

"Actually, we have squat," Simon says.

"Whaddaya—I mean how can you say that?"

Simon's phone pings, and a tiny soccer game flashes onto the screen. "Gotta go. So, right then . . ." Simon pivots.

"Wait a minute!" I grab his sleeve. "That's not fair. What about *us* mates?"

"Noah." Simon now sounds like he's talking to a little kid he feels sorry for. "I'll tell you what. Tomorrow we'll do something—take a canoe ride or something, all right?"

"But you saw the video! You heard the stories! You saw the Rottweilers!" I say that last part in a whisper.

Simon sighs sharply and rolls his eyes. "I saw an old recording with poor sound quality. I talked to George and your pops, who aren't the most reliable sources. Mike and Jake are stealing some stuff. So what? I have more important things to think about right now."

We stare at each other for a few seconds, neither

one of us wanting to be the one who blinks. Somewhere over the lake, a lone loon makes one of those weird, high-pitched loony laughs.

"Yeah, well, guess what?" I finally say, surprised by how angry Simon's made me. "Your important things are in another country, thousands of miles away. You're here. And probably will be for a long time. And here is here. Here is real!"

"You know what your problem is?" Simon retorts. "You don't know even what real is. Plus, you're a colossal pain in my—"

Simon stops abruptly and chews his cheek like he's trying hard to restrain himself. His gaze shifts off toward the lake.

"Good luck saving the world," he finally says. I watch him turn and trot back up the path, and when he's gone, I watch the nothing where he was. And I stand like that for about five minutes.

The night is darker now. I check the time, jog up the path, and squint into the woods.

Where is everyone? Have they all deserted me? Do they all think, like Simon, that our quest is rubbish? Or, worse than that, are they really not my mates?

Maybe Simon is right. Maybe I don't live in the real world. What if I'm not real? What if I live in an alternate reality or I'm someone else's dream? I pinch myself to make sure I exist, and it hurts. Also standing all tense and still in the bushes has made the muscles in my thighs ache, so chances are I'm real.

My thoughts are interrupted by a bunch of guffaws and snorts. From the other direction, Mike and Jake head toward the historic site.

CHAPTER 26

I hunker down and try to stay calm. I have to think. "*Think!* I mean it," I scold myself. "Think. Okay. Go!"

While I'm trying to decide what to think about, Mike and Jake come stomping down the path and start digging—grunting and thwacking into the dirt in rhythmic movements. They discover a few shards of this and that, grunt, pass the pieces back and forth, and chuck them into their sack.

Mike's phone rings. "Yeah, yeah," he says into the receiver.

It's their contact!

"Yeah, yeah, yeah." Mike's head bobs up and down.

"What?" Jake asks.

Mike holds his finger in the air, listens some more, and nods. "Yeah, got it, yeah," he says into the phone.

If only I could get closer to hear.

"What's he sayin'?" Jake asks.

Covering the receiver, Mike is like, "He says he knows where the valuable thing is. He says it took a long time, but now he's sure because he found the geonumeric coordinates."

Coordinates! I perk up.

"What's that?" Jake screws up his face.

"22, 44, 53," Mike answers.

"No, I mean, what are geo-whatever coordinates?"

"Um . . ." Mike furrows his brow.

"I'm confused," Jake says.

Finally, Mike is like, "Wait," as he holds his finger in front of Jake. "He's sending a map of the area."

A map of the area!

I watch them huddle around Mike's phone. Until someone taps my shoulder from behind. I jump.

"Sorry," Mia whispers. "Crystal from Bunk 12 asked me to sing for her Instagram. She has, like, a thousand followers. She also wants me to move into her bunk. Alice had to leave because she's allergic to macramé hemp. Then I couldn't find you. And I didn't want to use a flash—"

"Shhh!" I gesture toward the Rotts.

"Why didn't he tell us this before?" Jake says.

"He just got the intel," Mike answers. They've collected their stuff and are on the move. "Offa some old guys."

Mia's eyes and mine snap together.

Old guys!

"He says they're really cranky," Mike says.

"My grandpa gets cranky in Costco," Jake replies. "Loses it just when the cart is full and they're in the checkout line. Drives my mom ballistic."

"The boss says he had to restrain them," Mike says, barely audible now, as they head further into the brush. "Ya know, tie them up."

"Cool . . ." Jake's voice trails off.

Tie them up?!

Mia and I crouch-run through the brush after them. It's not easy because it's dark and the brush is scratchy and my entire legs are throbbing now. I'm super glad I sprayed myself with Bug Off, at least.

"Where's everyone else?" Mia whispers.

I shrug. I must look sad because Mia frowns and places her hand on my shoulder.

"'S'all right," she says.

And even though I'm disappointed about my mates and the world and stuff, it feels really good to have Mia with me.

Using the bright moonlight and low phone light, we make our way to the next clearing, near a small rundown shack. I don't know where I am now, but I hear some road traffic not far off in the distance.

Mike and Jake resume digging right next to a thick weeping willow tree.

And that's when a familiar voice rings out.

"Don't push! Dagnabbit!"

Pops stumbles out from behind the trees, looking small and angular, his hands fastened behind his back.

"Yeah, you better not untie my hands," George warns, shuffling behind, his glasses sliding down his nose. "'Cause if they weren't tied, I'd slap you silly."

Someone else glides behind them, wearing a long green trench coat and a hat pulled low over his head. His hands are shoved deep into his pockets.

"That must be the big boss," I whisper to Mia, craning my neck to see.

"Stay down," she whispers back. "We can't just rush in. We need a plan."

"We need mates," I say.

"We're war veterans!" George bellows. "We're used to torture."

"And I was a secret agent," Pops growls. "Liplock Field. I'm not telling anyone anything."

Trench Coat Guy moves past them as if he doesn't see anyone.

The thud of a shovel hits something hard. Dropping to his knees, Mike digs in the dirt with his hands.

"I think—yeah—this must be it!" Mike grunts, tugging a large piece of pottery from the earth.

"Hey, careful!" Jake offers a hand to help him.

Pops and George struggle against their restraints.

"You break it, you buy it!" Pops erupts.

Ignoring him, Trench Coat Guy steps around Jake. He crouches beside the hole and carefully tugs the clay slab from the ground. Cradling it in one hand, he gingerly dusts the dirt from it with the other. His hat slips back.

"It's Yipsy!" Mia says a little too loudly.

"Who's there?" Yipsy's head snaps around.

"Hey, it's Turtle!" Mike exclaims, wading into the bushes and grabbing my arm.

"Get his girlfriend too!" Jake yells.

I struggle against him. "Leave my girlfriend alone—er, you are my girlfriend, right?"

"Not now, Noah," Mia says, stumbling forward.

"Run, Ned!" Pops shrieks.

"What are you two doing here?" Yipsy asks.

"The question is, what are *you* doing here?" I demand.

"Probably the same thing you are," Yipsy says.

"I doubt that," I snap. "We're here to save the world, and you're here to steal!"

"No, little dude," Yipsy says. "It's not what it looks like."

"I told you kids, you can't trust hippies!" Pops announces.

Just then we hear a loud snap and the crunching of twigs and branches, not to mention a lot of grunting and swearing.

Josh and Tyler burst from the woods, panting. Gauze bandages in pops of bright white hang loosely around their arms. They look like badly wrapped Halloween mummies.

"Where were you?" I exclaim. "What happened?"

"Um . . . we had a little accident with the fire pit lighter fluid," Josh says.

"Scorched the hair off our arms," Tyler interjects. "And singed Josh's eyebrows."

"See?" Josh gestures to his bare forehead.

Mike and Jake exchange telepathic Neanderthal glances and march forward in unison. One grabs Josh while the other grabs Tyler.

"Hey!" Josh exclaims. "Hands off!"

The Rottweilers push Josh and Tyler over to us. We're all standing in front of the large, dark hole—the thing that held the thing that's going to save the world.

"What's he got?" Josh asks, gesturing toward Yipsy.

"The tablet," George grumbles.

"Is that really it?" Tyler asks, sliding forward. "It's pretty cool."

"I know, right?" Mike says. "It's heavy, too."

"It looks heavy." Tyler nods. "Can I touch it?"

Mike shrugs. "I guess."

Tyler extends his fingers and gently touches the clay. "Grainy," he says.

"This is totally a teaching moment!" Yipsy smiles. "Gather around and touch it. Don't worry, it doesn't bite."

"What in tarnation are you hippies doing?!" Pops explodes. "Give me that tablet!"

Our eyes slide to Pops's bound hands.

"Untie me and give me that tablet! We have to get it to Washington! To the president!"

We all exchange skeptical glances.

"Well, maybe not him," Pops grumbles. "But somebody in Washington!"

"Somebody who's not gonna steal the tablet for profit," George adds. "Like you!"

"Me?" Yipsy slaps his hand to his chest in disbelief.

And suddenly, as if just noticing Pops and George are tied up, he rushes to untie them. "Who did this?" he shouts furiously.

"We need to go to Atlantic City!" Pops says.

George leans in to Pops's ear. "Washington."

"That's what I meant," Pops grumbles.

"So you're not the bad guy?" George narrows his eyes at Yipsy.

"Bad guy? No," Yipsy says. "Of course not. I'm just trying to instill values in these kids: teach them, nurture them, encourage them to find themselves— at least until mid-August."

"Do you even know what you got there, son?" George asks.

"Of course I do. It's a valuable historical artifact, which these bananas," Yipsy says scoldingly, gesturing to Mike and Jake, "have been stealing and selling online."

"We're just 'Showing Our Stuff,'" Mike sneers, making quotation marks in the air and elbowing Jake. "Get it?"

"No," Jake says flatly.

"What you're showing," Yipsy says to the Rott-weilers, getting all red-in-the-face annoyed, "is that you need a few good lessons in the bad karma of stealing."

"You tell 'em, Yipsy!" Mia urges.

While Yipsy yaks on about karma and life lessons, Pops sneaks around him and gently extracts the tablet from his hands.

"Well, we'll just be moseying along now." He turns and nods to everyone. "Nice to see you, Hippie. Trolls, Oaf-y boys, Girl . . . Come on, Ned."

He's about to shuffle away when Mike is like, "Stop right there, old guy. You ain't going anywhere."

"And who in tarnation is gonna stop me?" Pops exclaims.

Mike steps into Pops's path.

"Hey, back off!" Josh shouts.

Mike glowers at Josh and slams his shovel hard into the ground. Jake holds his shovel across his chest like a weapon.

"Um . . . please," Josh says as he and Tyler retreat.

"Wait one minute," Yipsy says. "What is so bleepin' important about that particular clay tablet? Excuse my language."

"You should know," Pops says. "You're the one tryin' to steal it."

"Didn't you just hear a word I said?" Yipsy answers, throwing his hands up in exasperation.

This whole thing has gone wonky! It's time for me to start saving the world.

And I'm ready. My stomach doesn't even hurt, and I feel pretty pumped up about it.

"Yipsy," I say in my most commanding voice, "this tablet was transcribed by World War II Navajo code talkers. It's encoded with the coordinates to save us from a rogue asteroid named Agatha that is going destroy the earth in exactly"—I check the time on my phone—"sometime soon. And it's up to us to get it to Washington so we can save the world."

"Say what now?" Yipsy looks confused.

"So," I conclude, taking the tablet from Pops, "we gotta get out of here."

At that moment, a large, dark figure steps out from behind the black, shadowy trees.

"Stop right there! No one is getting out of here."

CHAPTER 27

"Who's that?" Josh asks, squinting into the darkness.

"Is it . . . ?" I cautiously slide closer.

"What's going on?" Yipsy asks.

"That's the big hairy guy who tied us up!" Pops exclaims.

From out of the gloom steps the imposing figure of Nurse Leibowitz.

"Hey, that's no guy!" George grumbles.

She's wearing one of her usual velour track outfits, this one in green, along with her medical fanny pack belted on her ample hips like a holster from the OK Corral. From behind her back, she pulls out a big red fire extinguisher and points it right at us!

"Um, whatcha doin', Nurse Leibowitz?" I ask.

"Shut up!" she roars, swinging the hose at me, spritzing white gunk onto the ground at my feet.

"Hey!" I shout, jumping backward.

"Get back!" she yells, narrowing her eyes, moving toward us, slowly swinging the nozzle from one of us to the next.

"Nurse Leibowitz," Yipsy says, "what's going on? Who's watching the kids? Where's the fire?"

"I'm coming after you, you outdated weirdo," Nurse Leibowitz snarls. "I came for the tablet. The kids are writing family emails and are engaged in constructive social-media-free time, and there's no fire, you nitwit! So give me that tablet," she orders, lunging toward me.

"Um . . . no?" I say.

"Atta boy, Ned!" Pops pumps his fist in the air.

"Listen, Myrna," Yipsy says gently. "I don't know what's going on, but this kooky, menacing behavior—this isn't you. Is it, kids?"

There's a beat of silence.

"Kids?" Yipsy sings, popping his eyes wide and wiggling his eyebrows at us.

"No," "Totally not," "Of course not," "Pfffft," "Not at all," we overlap each other.

"Well, it kind of is . . ." Josh mumbles, and Tyler jabs him in the ribs.

Yipsy moves slowly toward Nurse Leibowitz, his

arms outstretched like he's a dad who wants his turn to cuddle the baby fire extinguisher.

"Now, Myrna," he coos. "All this nonsense . . . it's just the fire pit charcoal's carbon monoxide fumes talking. You know what you need? A good old-fashioned wheatgrass cleanse, a relaxing nap in the hemp hammock, maybe some therapy . . ."

I hold my breath. Yipsy's fingers are just about to make contact with the cylinder when—

"I. Said. Don't!" Nurse Leibowitz explodes, hitting him with a full spray of fire extinguisher gunk until he's covered from head to toe in what looks like a layer of white marshmallow.

"Uhhgghhlllll!!" Yipsy garbles, wiping his eyes, spitting, and trying to shake the stuff off.

And we're all like, "Gross!" "Disgusting!" "Jeez!" "Gag." "It's like white snot!"

Nurse Leibowitz leaps at me and snatches the tablet from my hands.

"Hey!" I try to grab it back, but she threatens me with the hose.

"Who's this loony bird?" Pops asks.

"That's the camp nurse," Tyler says.

"That's no nurse," Pops says. "She must be a secret agent."

"You're right about that, old man." Nurse Leibowitz throws back her head and cackles. "I am a secret agent."

"Who do you work for?" George asks.

"It's a secret!"

George and Pops nod conspiratorially.

"Oh my God," Josh says. "They're, like, bonding or something."

"Grab her, Mike! Jake!" Yipsy yells.

But she aims the nozzle at them, and they back up.

"This is getting too weird," Mike says. "A good boss always knows when it's time to let his subordinates take the fall. I'm outta here."

"Me too," Jake says.

"No!" Myrna yells. "No witnesses."

"I don't understand," Josh whispers. "She can't take us all. And that white stuff isn't toxic."

"Excuse me, but it totally is," Mia says. "It murders the ozone."

Josh rolls his eyes. "And we included her *why*?"

Mike and Jake catch each other's eyes and sprint for the trees.

"Come back! Come back!" Nurse Leibowitz yells, pointing the fire extinguisher at them. "No witnesses!"

Mike stops abruptly and swivels around. "We won't rat you out," Mike says.

Jake nods. "We can't."

"And may I ask why not?" Nurse Leibowitz puts her hand on her hip.

"Because, hello." Mike holds up his shovel and burlap sack. "Stealing."

"Oh. Right," she says. "Then you can go."

Mike and Jake bolt faster than I thought they could move.

"What do you want with the tablet, Nurse Leibowitz?" I ask. "Are you trying to save the world?"

"Save the world?" She cocks her head. "What are you talking about?"

"*Tikun olam!* Repairing the world? Doing a mitzvah? Bringing light into the spiritual realm? Ari the Lion?" I rattle off sharply.

At that moment, we hear the cracking of branches coming from behind Nurse Leibowitz. A voice says, "You didn't have to scare me to death, sneaking up on me in Noah's cabin."

And a second voice: "I wasn't sneaking."

The first voice again: "This muck will totally ruin my new sneakers!"

The second voice, sounding irritated: "Do stop complaining, won't you?"

I'd know that American whining and that British scolding anywhere. It's Lily and Simon!

Nurse Leibowitz's head snaps toward the voices. It's time for me to distract her.

"Nurse Leibowitz!" I yell. "I think I have poison ivy!"

She spins around, her nurse autopilot kicking in. "Well, don't scratch it!" she commands, rummaging through her black bag. "You'll just make it worse. We need Neosporin and a compress and—"

"What are you guys doing here?" Simon asks, stepping out from the trees, looking perplexed. "We had a devil of a time finding you. Noah, I owe you an apology, mate, and—"

"Grab Nurse Leibowitz! She's the bad guy!" I yell.

Nurse Leibowitz spins and kicks Simon in the side. "HIYAH!"

"OOF!" Simon exhales. "What the—that hurt!" he yells, as she windmills toward him.

"Hey!" Lily shouts and shoves Nurse Leibowitz hard, sending her stumbling back.

Nurse Leibowitz sets her laser eyes on Lily and

lunges for her. Simon jumps in front of Lily while bobbing and ducking blows from Nurse Leibowitz's windmill arms.

"She's totally out of control!" Simon yells.

"You got that right, hippie!" Pops shouts, as he and George shadowbox the air.

Simon manages to grab Nurse Leibowitz from behind and wrestle her to the ground. I grab the fire extinguisher. Nurse Leibowitz struggles, screams, and kicks.

"A little help here," Simon pants, struggling desperately to hold on to her.

"She's doing Krav Maga!" Pops shouts.

Nurse Leibowitz throws Simon off and leaps to her feet.

"HIYAH!" she howls while slicing her hands through the air.

Yipsy jumps into the fray and throws his arms around her shoulders, but she slips from his grasp and shoves him hard against a tree.

"My leg!" he shouts.

I'm sliding around trying to get a variety of angles on film. Talk about good footage!

"Noah, what have you gotten yourself into?" Lily bobs and weaves. "I am so telling Mom and Dad."

She and Mia lunge at Nurse Leibowitz, trying to grab her, but she does some kind of jump-spin-kick, knocking them both to the ground.

"HIYAH!" Nurse Leibowitz shouts again.

Josh and Tyler dance around Nurse Leibowitz in sumo wrestler stances, trying to find a way in.

"Jump on her!" Simon shouts.

"Dude, I'm not jumping on her," Josh says.

"Me neither," Tyler agrees.

"Noah!" Simon yells.

Suddenly, a disoriented-looking person stumbles out from the bushes.

"Hey, Nathan!" I shout breathlessly, dancing around the chaos. "Duck!"

"What the—?" Nathan ducks as his shocked face darts from one person to the next. "What's going on here?"

"Long story. I'll explain later, but just roll with it," I suggest, hopping around. "But now that you're here, I have some questions. I thought saving the world would be noble. Like, I'd be in a parade or on the news or something. Or it would be cool—like, I'd be in a car chase film sequence. I never thought it would be about trying to capture a nutty nurse in the middle of the woods at Camp Challah. You're a deep thinker who knows a lot about Judaism. In your opinion, what would Moses do?"

"WHHHAAAT?!" Nathan shouts incredulously, scrambling behind a tree.

"Noah!" Simon yells, trying to extract himself from Nurse Leibowitz's headlock.

"Fine . . . I'll do it!" I yell and leap right onto her back. She spins around and tries to swat me, but I have a good hold, with one hand over her eyes.

"Ah! I can't see!" she bellows. "HIYAH! HIYAH!" she screams. "Let go!"

"Sorry, Nurse Leibowitz." My words vibrate as I bounce wildly. "It's time to calm down and use your inside voice!"

"Inside voice *this!*" she yells and throws herself back hard, slamming me against a tree.

A sharp pain explodes across my spine, and I crash into a heap on the ground.

"Noah!" Lily shouts and runs toward me. "Are you okay?"

"Maybe," I wheeze, the wind knocked out of me.

She helps pull me upright. "Simon told me what you've been up to, Noah," she says. "And before the world ends, I want you to know that you don't totally bite as a brother. I mean, I'm not completely embarrassed by you *all* the time."

"Thanks, Lily," I say, surprised. "That's really nice, ya know, for you."

"But if we get out of this alive, I'm totally gonna kill you," she adds.

"Noah, are you all right?" Nathan gingerly joins our circle. "Yipsy, what's happening?"

"'S'all right, Nathan," Yipsy says gently, eyeballing Nurse Leibowitz and sliding in front of us. "I've got everything under control . . . ish. Oh, and it would be cool if you didn't tell your dad about this."

Nurse Leibowitz stands triumphantly. Behind her, the sky lightens in gradations of the soft pinks and blues of early dawn, illuminating her silhouette like the best movie backdrop I've ever seen!

"Now maybe you'll understand that I mean business!" she pants, reaching into fanny pack and extracting a . . . something pointy.

"Whoa!" Yipsy exclaims, holding his hands in the air.

"Shut up!" She points the thing at him.

I lean toward Simon. "What is that?" I ask quietly out of the corner of my mouth.

"It looks like a high-tech bow and arrow," Josh whispers.

"I think it's called a crossbow," Simon says. "I saw one in the archery shed. We aren't allowed to use it."

"It looks sharp," Josh notes.

"You're darn tootin' it's sharp!" Nurse Leibowitz announces.

"Kids, step back," Yipsy says. "Myrna, violence isn't the answer."

"Since when?" she snarls, her eyes aglow. "Now, you're going to give me that tablet. I'm gonna walk out of here, and you're going to give me a twenty-minute lead. Then you're going to forget you ever saw me. If you don't, well—you'll see then, won't you?"

We all look confused.

"What will we see?" I ask.

"I'll . . . plaster all your embarrassing personal information on social media!"

"What?" "Huh?" "What's she talking about?" we all say at the same time.

"I know everything about you." She nods smugly. "Your immunizations, your allergies, your weird dietary restrictions, your revolting whiny neuroses: 'I don't like elevators,'" she says in a pretend whiny voice. "'Cilantro in my Tex Mex food tastes like soap.' 'I'm afraid of scary-looking dolls.' 'Roller coasters make me nauseous.' *I can ruin your lives!*"

Nurse Leibowitz cackles. "And don't think I won't!"

"You know what I think?" George explodes. "I think it's time to shut your trap, lady!"

"Shut yours, old man!" Nurse Leibowitz slants her eyes at him.

"You don't even know what you got there, do you?" he says, gesturing to the tablet.

"An extremely rare and valuable artifact," she answers haughtily.

"That's not all, Fruit Loops," Pops says.

"The tablet gives exact instructions about how to save the world from a killer asteroid," I tell her. "If you don't give that to us, then in exactly about two weeks' time the whole world will be blown to bits."

"I don't believe you." Nurse Leibowitz glances at the tablet. "How do you know?"

"My cousin Bobby Running Feather was a code talker during World War II," George says, jabbing his finger at her, "and he wrote that tablet."

"I know a Bobby Running Feather." Nurse Leibowitz cocks her head. "Was he with the Navajo Nation?"

"Yeah," George narrows his eyes at her, skeptically.

"He was my fourth cousin!"

"Uh, Leibowitz?" Simon poses the question.

"On my mother's side," she snaps.

"I don't believe you." George crosses his arms over his chest.

"It's true," she says, all steely. "I did a cheek swab DNA test. Once I discovered that, I decided to learn the Navajo language and wartime codebook!"

"You're lyin'." George scowls.

"I'll prove it to you," Nurse Leibowitz says. She sets the crossbow down next to her feet and squints at the tablet.

"Wait a minute now," she says, fumbling through her fanny pack. "I just need my reading glasses. I really should get one of those necklace chains, but they're so old-fogey-looking—no offense." She nods to George and Pops. "Ah, here we go!" she says, wiggling her face into the little purple glasses.

She starts to read.

"Uh-huh . . . uh-huh . . . hmmm," she mumbles. "Oh, that's funny." She throws back her head and cackles. "Uh-huh . . . Wow, interesting . . ."

"Any day now, Mixed Nuts." Pops taps his foot.

"Oh! Oh no! Oh no! Terrible, terrible . . . OMG!"

"She really has lost it." Lily rolls her eyes condescendingly. "Nobody says OMG anymore."

"This is very, very bad!" Nurse Leibowitz finally exclaims, whipping off her glasses.

"I told you so!" George says.

"Now give us the doggone tablet so we can save the world!" Pops demands.

"It's very bad for you." Nurse Leibowitz grins, which makes her look even scarier. "But very good for me! Do you know what I can get for this tablet?"

"You can't spend the money if we're all dead, Loony Bird!" Pops says.

"Oh yeah? Just watch me!" Nurse Leibowitz laughs maniacally.

Mia catches my eye and gestures to the crossbow on the ground. I'm the closest to it. Can I grab it? Do I have the nerve?

Simon nods in an encouraging way, or at least I think that's what he's doing. Maybe it isn't. Maybe it's a rhetorical nod, or maybe he's agreeing with Pops. Or maybe he just likes to nod. And what if Nurse Leibowitz grabs the weapon first? What if the arrow hits me and it hurts—a lot?

Simon is grimacing now with a more aggressive head bounce in the direction of the crossbow.

Very cautiously, I inch forward.

"So, um tell me, Nurse Leibowitz." Simon shifts to her other side in what I think is an effort to distract her. "Have, um, you always wanted to be a nurse?"

"What?"

"I mean, what, um, led you to want to help people?"

"What in tarnation is that hippie talking about?" Pops mutters.

"Well, I . . ." Nurse Leibowitz looks like she's processing and trying to read Simon's room, while I creep closer and closer to the crossbow, which gleams in the oncoming gray dusk of pre-dawn. "Whaddaya mean?" she asks skeptically.

"Well," Simon says, shifting slowly away from me, so that her head turns toward him. "You're such a brilliant nurse, and I was wondering what led you to a life of healing."

"Oh." Nurse Leibowitz blushes and gets really serious. "Yes. I always wanted to help people. Even as a child."

"You don't say?" Simon looks super interested. "Tell me more about that."

Closer. Closer. This is the scariest thing I've ever done. I feel the others holding their breath. Simon glances my way and shoots me an encouraging, tight smile. Lily looks teary but nods encouragingly.

"I had a dog named Wags," Nurse Leibowitz says. "And I remember being about maybe three and putting a stethoscope to his heart, and then trying to give him CPR with our old ping-pong paddles. But then my parents made me stop—and then they sent Wags away to live with my cousin after that." She dabs at her eyes. "I don't know why. I was heartbroken. Until I noticed that my cat's tail looked curly and broken, so I decided to straighten it, but then my parents sent her away too, and . . ."

Crouching very slowly, I reach out, and my fingers graze the cold steel. I've almost got it! Suddenly, my headpiece camera buzzes and flashes a red light, indicating that I'm running out of space.

"HEY!" Nurse Leibowitz pivots.

Like lightning, she grabs for the weapon. But I've already curled my fingers around the handle and have it firmly in my clutches. We struggle, and everything around me is a blur. I see the terrified faces of my family and my mates. And from the corner of my eye, I see Lily on her phone.

CHAPTER 28

Nurse Leibowitz is throwing me around and twisting my arm, but I won't let go. Because this is my chance to do something really important and save the world and, also, I don't want to get hurt.

Finally, I wrench the crossbow away from her.

And now I'm standing with this sharp weapon, pointing it at her, and she's standing there in front of me and it's, like, who am I?

"Don't move!" I yell. "Or I'll—"

Oh my God, what will I do?!

"You'll what?" Nurse Leibowitz snickers. "That crossbow couldn't hurt a fly."

"What?" Simon exclaims.

"I work at a camp with *children*, for God's sake. I totally sanded down the arrow tip. See? I even glued rubber over it."

While we're all trying to figure out how to respond to this, Nurse Leibowitz holds up the tablet.

"You'll never catch me!" she cackles. "And you can't prove any of this!"

"Oh, yes, we can," I say in a really stern voice that I didn't know I had. "Because I"—I tilt my head down—"got it all on film, which will one day be my new opus."

"You still got pus?" Pops asks.

Nurse Leibowitz looks kind of shocked. Her face droops, and her mouth opens and closes like she's gonna says something, but she just looks like a fish who can't get air.

Lily lifts the tablet from her hands. "That's what you get for being evil *and* wearing last decade's athleisure wear."

At that moment, police sirens whine up the road. The cars screech to a stop. Car doors open and slam. The sounds of voices and stampeding feet head our way.

"We're down here, officers!" Yipsy yells. Before she can bolt, we surround Nurse Leibowitz like a human cage.

"Is this you saving the world?" Nathan asks, dumbfounded.

"It looks that way," I reply.

A bunch of police officers rush down the embankment. I place the crossbow on the ground, and we all start talking over each other. The police confer with Yipsy—even though they don't seem completely convinced that he's a reliable witness, since he's covered in hardening, cracking white goo. But, somehow, they manage to get most of the story. Yipsy offers to accompany them down to the station to fill in the details.

"I'll come too," Nathan says, still looking totally confused, like he accidentally walked into the carnival funhouse in someone else's nightmare.

The officers handcuff Nurse Leibowitz. Just as they're about to haul her off, she cranes her head over her shoulder, looks straight at me, and shouts, "One zero one four five one!"

And giggles.

I'm too tired to even wonder what that's supposed to mean.

It's almost dawn now. Somewhere in the distance, birds chirp, and the woods are alive with the sounds of cricket-y, croaking, woodsy things. The sky is fading to yellow-white as a light breeze blows in from the lake. In the distance, I hear the muffled sounds of kids. Camp Challah is waking up.

George, Pops, my mates, and I stand in the small clearing in the big woods. Nobody seems to know what to do or say.

"Wow," Tyler finally says.

"You were awesome, Noah," Mia tells me.

"It was nothing," I reply with a shrug.

"No, really," she insists. "You were epic. Like, song-worthy epic."

I'm embarrassed to feel a hot blush crawl up my neck and onto my cheeks.

"Glad that's over," says Josh with a weary sigh. "I'm starving."

"Aren't you forgetting something?" Simon asks.

"What's that?" Tyler says.

My eyes meet Simon's.

We say it together: "We still have to save the world."

CHAPTER 29

"I thought you didn't even believe in Agatha and saving the world," I say to Simon.

"Well," he sighs, "I didn't. But I should believe in *you*. I thought about everything you've done and said. And I realize I kind of admire you. You're my best mate here in the States, after all. And it doesn't look like I'm leaving anytime soon."

This is amazing! I have a best friend who thinks I'm cool.

"I'm glad to hear you say that, mate! That's great!" I say. "Great mate. Great mate. Ha ha, that rhymes . . . But seriously, mate is a cool word. Much nicer than friend. Frieeenddd." I move my mouth around that word until it sounds all nasally and uncool. "Frieeeeennnnnd. But mate—much better. Mate, mate, mate," I singsong in a crisp, clipped way.

"Noah." Lily shuts me down.

"Sorry. Tired."

"Aren't we all," George says, lowering himself onto a rock with a long groan.

"Well, I'm not," Pops declares, carefully cradling the tablet. "We still need to get to Washington. George, call an Uber. We're going to the airport. But first, we're stopping at the diner, 'cause I got the bathroom hoppies. We're gonna wait by the road. Wish us luck."

"Shouldn't we go with them?" Simon asks quietly.

"Don't worry," Pops says. "Those young whippersnappers in Washington have to listen to us now that we have the tablet. Besides, George is a decorated World War II veteran, and I was a . . ."

"Secret agent," we all drone in unison.

"That's right!" Pops exclaims.

"But there's still a chance the asteroid will blow us to bits," Josh says. "It would be nice to grow up."

"Yeah, it would," Simon agrees. "Play football."

"Write sci-fi shows," Tyler adds.

"Write more songs!" Mia nods.

"Yeah . . . about that," Josh says.

"Not cool." Mia glowers at him for a moment

before she turns to me. "You think we'll get to do any of those things, Noah?"

"Hmmm," I reply absentmindedly. I'm not really paying attention because something's nagging at the back of my mind.

"Pops, come back here a minute," I say.

"What is it? Every second counts when you're trying to save the world and you've got the bathroom hoppies."

"What were those numbers Nurse Leibowitz rattled off?" I say, both to myself and rhetorically.

"Who cares?" Josh says. "Let's head back to camp. Carbs. Now."

Everyone starts toward the lake. I remove my camera headpiece and rewind it.

"One zero one four five one," Nurse Leibowitz chortles. "One zero one four five one!"

I play it a few times: *101451.*

"Noah, you're obsessing again," Lily says.

"No. Wait. Pops, do those numbers mean anything to you? George?"

George shrugs. "Nope."

I repeat the numbers a few more times. "Six numbers. Maybe they're groups."

"Or pairs?" Lily adds.

"Or dates," I say, the meaning slowly dawning on me. "The dates the asteroid will hit."

Simon gently lifts the tablet from Pops's hands and lays it down on a flat rock. We cluster around it. I readjust my headpiece and hit *Record*.

We stare in silence for a few seconds, boring our eyes into the tablet.

Josh breaks the silence. "You know we can't read this, right?"

"Sure, but if it's a date, then it's October 14, 1951," I say, thinking aloud. "So that means—"

"It happened already," Lily says, plopping down on a rock and crossing her legs.

"But we're still here," Josh says.

"So . . . it's all bogus?" Tyler grazes his fingers across the tablet as if the truth will somehow jump up his hand and slide into his brain.

"Now, just a minute, kids," George pipes up. "This is the real McCoy here."

"It might be the real McCoy, whatever that means," Simon says. "But it could be an *old* McCoy."

"It says here," Lily reads from her phone, "that in October 1951, scientists predicted that a great asteroid would destroy Earth. The giant asteroid, named Agatha, was approximately two-and-a-half kilometers in size. The information was corroborated by the world community of scientists, amateur astronomers, astrologists and Native American Earth Watch groups. Fortunately for Earth's inhabitants, once Agatha entered Earth's atmosphere, she shattered, and the largest pieces dropped into the Antarctic Sea. What some saw as a random close call for mankind, others saw as an act of divine intervention."

We all listen in astonished silence.

"Bobby Running Feather, a decorated World War II veteran and code talker, believed the asteroid's approach wasn't just a random act of nature. 'It was a warning for us to learn to coexist in peace and tolerance and not waste our natural resources or destroy our great Mother Earth.'"

"I love him!" Mia gushes.

"When asked why he thinks we dodged the bullet, he simply said, 'Our ability to rally and unify has given us another chance.' Whether you call it luck or divine intervention or cosmic warning, the earth spins on to meet another day."

"Well, I'll be darned." Pops shakes his head. "We missed it."

"It missed us," I correct him.

"WE LIVE!" Tyler exclaims.

"Time for chow!" Josh says, leading us back toward Camp C. We fall in line behind him.

"I have so many songs in my head," Mia says. "Need. My. Guitar. Now."

Josh groans.

"I heard that," Mia says as the group rounds the tall pine trees.

Somewhere on the road, an Uber honks its horn. George starts the slow climb up the hill.

Pops sinks down onto a rock and stares quietly into space.

"You comin'?" George asks over his shoulder.

"In a minute," Pops says.

George nods and vanishes into the trees.

CHAPTER 30

"What's up, Pops?" I say, slipping into the indented curve on the rock beside him. It's full-on morning now. Birds sing, and I hear the happy sounds of Camp Challah in the distance.

I should be exhausted, but I feel funny. Not ha-ha funny but *different* funny, like peaceful and happy but maybe a little sad, too.

Pops doesn't say anything, so I take a stab at reading his room. "I guess you're kind of disappointed."

He shrugs. "'Bout what?"

"About, like, the false alarm and everything."

"It happens," he says.

"You didn't get to go to Washington, but it was still kind of a big adventure."

"True," he remarks.

"You know," I say, "it's been my experience that

263

sometimes you plan for one thing and then some-thing else comes along, and it's almost better. You know what I mean?"

"No."

"Like, for example," I continue, "I really wanted to go to the David Lynch Film Camp."

"To be a stylist," Pops nods. "I remember."

"Um, yeah. Well, I didn't get to go and, at first, I was really disappointed. But if I had gone, none of this would have happened. I wouldn't have all this in the can." I tap the camera on my head. "That's film talk for having good stuff on film."

"You can still do ladies' hair, Ned." Pops pats my shoulder.

"No, I mean—"

Pops pulls himself to his feet, picks up the tablet, and starts climbing up toward the road. I follow.

"I'm fine," he says. "You go back to camp."

"I'll walk with you."

"I'm fine," he repeats.

All sorts of thoughts run through my head. Is he fine? Is he being rhetorical? Is he sad? Does he really think I want to be a hair stylist, or is he messing with me? Does he know me at all? Sometimes I wish he would just make more sense.

"Pops," I say, frustrated, "I can't figure out what you're feeling."

He stops and turns, and the sun hits him full on. As if seeing him for the first time, I notice the deep wrinkles around his eyes, the thinness of his cotton-candy white hair, and those brown splotchy age spots on his hands. Like Agatha the asteroid, one day all that will be left of Pops will be a strange memory.

"Noah." Pops faces me. "You're a good kid."

"Thanks, Pops."

"So you want to be a filmmaker?" he continues.

"Well—yeah. You got it right."

"That's nice," he says, his twinkly eyes meeting mine. "You'll be good at it."

"What makes you say that?"

"You see the truth in people. That's good for an artsy kid. And you're caring. And I like your friends, even if they are hippies and trolls. And they like you."

"Thanks."

"I had a good time," he says. "A good adventure. I'm glad I did this now."

"Did this now?" I ask. "Whaddaya mean?"

"You'll get it. One day. Maybe when you have a grandson. Someone like you," he says, and the tiniest bit of a smile tugs the corners of his mouth.

Did Pops set this all in motion on purpose? Maybe to help me? I think that's something I'll never know. Maybe I don't really need to know.

"Yeah," Pops sighs. "Maybe George and I will go to Washington anyways. I'll bring this. They should know about it. Important historical artifact and all that. They oughta know the proper channels to get it back to the Navajo Nation."

"That's a great idea," I agree.

He turns to go, and I want to say so much more. But I don't exactly know what—or where to start.

"So, will I see you soon?" I ask, settling for that.

"Well, after Washington, George and I will probably go to Atlantic City. Then I'm off to Florida, and then we'll see. I'm a busy man . . . Noah."

The Uber horn honks more urgently.

"I'm coming, dagnabbit!" he yells.

And with that, he hobbles up the soft slope of the hill, muttering cranky stuff to himself the whole way, until he's gone from view.

CHAPTER 31

The rest of the summer at Camp C flies by.

Nathan has been anxious to know what was going on in the woods that night. So during the last campfire marshmallow roast, I tell him everything.

"Well, I can honestly say," he says with a grin, stabbing a marshmallow onto a stick, "that's a strange story. But whaddaya gonna do now that you won't be saving the world from an asteroid? I mean, for your Bar Mitzvah project?"

I need to think about that one. Flipping on my head camera, I sweep the scene. Kids are everywhere, happily flitting in and out of the firelight in what looks like an improvised dance. We've all made new mates. And if it isn't forever, at least the memories will last a long time. I'm glad I'll have so many of them on film.

"I dunno," I sigh, poking at the campfire embers with my stick. "Maybe I can make a documentary about . . . friendship. Would that work?"

"Well." Nathan looks solemn, wiping his sticky hands on his shorts. "Observing and documenting is a way of contributing to the world. For example, there are lots of kids who can't afford good things like going to camp. Maybe you can make a documentary about that."

"Yeah," I agree, suddenly really engaged, feeling the way you do when something feels right. "I could make a *cinéma vérité* about kids in need. Ya know, raise awareness like Mia does with her songs. Maybe I could even raise money for them and stuff."

Nathan raises his palm for a high five. I still think high fives are super awkward, but I slap his hand anyway so he isn't insulted.

"Good call," he says, grinning. "Moses would be proud."

"Say what now?" From out of nowhere, Janine plops down on our log next to Nathan. She smiles broadly, her super-white teeth and blond hair glowing in the firelight. "Moses would be proud?"

"I . . ." Nathan freezes, his eyes go glossy, and his mouth pulls down like he just tasted something sour.

"Ajekekf . . ." he mumbles, moving his hand to his mouth, then down again, then up to scratch his head.

"Speak English," I whisper. "And put your hands down. Breathe. You can do it."

Nathan inhales and exhales loudly through his nose. "I was saying that Moses would be proud of this kid. It's a long story. Wanna hear it?"

"Sure," Janine says.

"Also"—he yanks a paperback from his pocket—"I have many interesting stories about the Kabbalah and about Rabbi Akiva from the first century."

"Um . . . okay." Janine sounds a little less sure.

I take that as my cue to exit stage right, and by the time I glance back at them from the DJ turntable, they're chatting easily like good mates.

Simon and Lily have been sort of dating, which means they sit next to each other at the evening campfires, share jokes, and flirt. She acts like she can take him or leave him, but I can tell she likes him a lot. He's been complaining that she's always with her mates, but he's mostly with *his* mates (us), so it works out pretty well.

Simon also hasn't forgotten about *tikkun olam* and Ari the Lion, and he's super interested in learning more. We've been spending some afternoons hanging out with Rabbi Blum, who continues to be super excited to explain it.

Tyler and Josh have become really good at Canoe Rowing for Lake Explorers. They even won the Color War title of Fastest Rowers in the History of Camp.

Mia has been writing lots of new songs and, to Yipsy's delight, has been "showing her stuff" like crazy. Now her verses are about asteroids and Mother Earth, with choruses about tolerance and peace. A few are even about me, whom she refers to as "the unlikely guy who would have saved the world from an asteroid if it needed saving."

I think she's my girlfriend, even though she says she doesn't like labels because they reduce people to social stereotypes. I don't feel reduced, but I like her a lot and know we'll be friends even after camp ends.

As anyone might guess, Nurse Leibowitz has been fired from camp. And even though she didn't get any time in the Big House, she has to do, like, three hundred hours of community service and get anger management counseling.

A few days after our adventure, I got a note from Pops attached to Sal. It said, *Be a Lover, Not a Fighter.*

I'm not really sure what it means, but it was nice to see Sal again.

About a week after that, I got some snail-mail from Pops. He sent me a cut-out newspaper article with the title "World War II Heroes find Significant Artifact."

Underneath the title is a grainy black-and-white picture of Pops and George holding the tablet and standing next to the head of artifacts at the Washington Museum. (I know this because Pops labeled everyone in the picture with small sticky notes, including himself and George.) They look happy.

The article talks about the tablet and about the contributions of code talkers. It also describes our skirmish with Nurse Leibowitz and praises Pops and George for their bravery. There's a small quote from Pops where he talks about his "brave grandson, Noah," which he highlighted in shaky lines with a yellow marker.

As for me, I've completed one of my documentaries, which I've titled *My Life So Far and How Cool It's Been Even Though I Didn't Really Save the World*. Mia says it's too long, but I kind of like it. I put it on YouTube, and it's starting to get hits!

And even though Mom and Dad aren't letting me go to the DLFC Extended Summer Program, they say they'll think about the DLFC Winter Break Two-Week Intensive Session. So I'm sending my opus along with the application. I hope I get in!

Wouldn't it be cool if I did and could wheedle a hard "yes" from Mom and Dad by Thanksgiving? That would mean I could spend the holidays in sunny Los Angeles!

I wonder what kind of adventure I'll have there.

ABOUT THE AUTHOR

Laura Toffler-Corrie is an award-winning author of young adult and middle-grade novels. She teaches creative writing and literature at Pace University. Laura lives in New York state with her husband, two daughters, and a variety of large and small animals. She enjoys the beach at twilight, museum crawls, and quoting dumb movies.

ABOUT THE ILLUSTRATOR

Macky Pamintuan was born and raised in the Southern Philippines. He received his Bachelor of Fine Arts degree from the Academy of Art College in San Francisco. In addition to illustrating, Macky enjoys playing basketball, his other true passion. He lives in the Philippines with his wife, their baby girl, and a West Highland white terrier named Winter.